age of shade

A STEAMY, FORBIDDEN, AGE GAP ROMANCE

CLEO WHITE

 Created with Vellum

Do you think the universe fights for souls to be together?

Some things are too strange and strong to be coincidences.

EMERY ALLEN

This book contains themes that may not be suitable to some readers. Please read with care.

Trigger Warnings: **Death of a parent (off page), mentions of drug abuse and drug overdose, physical abuse, neglect, depression and suicidal thoughts, and severe bullying (off page).**

ASHER

3 YEARS AGO

"DO YOU SEE, RIGHT BACK HERE?" I lean over so my patient's mother can peer into her son's mouth, narrowing her eyes to make out the reflection in the tiny mirror I'm holding.

"That's a *cavity*?" She winces, hurriedly sitting back in her chair with a chalk-white face.

Setting my tools on the tray table, I nod sympathetically. "It is. A pretty nasty one, too." I hand her son a small paper cup of water and he gulps it back greedily, looking relieved I'm no longer prodding and poking around in his mouth. "Fortunately, it's just a baby tooth. He would have lost it within the next year or two anyway, so I would recommend extraction in this case. It's really not worth filling it."

"Awesome. You're gonna rip out my tooth?" my patient, Guillermo, asks enthusiastically. "Can I have it after?"

I have to press my lips together to keep myself from

laughing out loud. "Sure, I'll keep it for you to give to the tooth fairy."

Guillermo pauses, considering. "Instead, can I hang it around my neck like a shark's tooth? It would *totally* freak out Jeremy and Trey."

Snapping my gloves off and tossing them toward the trash, I can't help but chuckle at his bright, hopeful expression. "I think that's a discussion you'll need to have with your mom." Glancing over at her, I see she's still pale, her face pinched together with worry. "It's a very minor, safe procedure. I have room in my schedule on Friday afternoon, so he wouldn't need to miss much school."

She nods slowly, chewing the inside of her cheek. "Do you know how much it will cost?"

My heart sinks. I'm currently the only pediatric dentist in this neighborhood, and it's not a mystery why. In this area of New York—a working-class corner of Harlem—hardly any of my patients have the luxury of dental insurance or parents who can take days off work and shell out thousands of dollars for surgeries. "I'll have my office manager work up an estimate for you before you leave. We do partner with a monthly payment service—"

She's already shaking her head, though, staring at the floor with embarrassment coloring her cheeks. "My credit is shit. You know how it is."

Yeah, I know exactly how it is. My mother raised my brother and me alone, with no help from the men who fathered us. She lives in Florida now, happily retired and living in a condo David and I purchased for her a few years back. We made it through, but I'll still never forget the days when the only full meal we got was at school, or what it was like to hear mom crying over a stack of bills at the kitchen table when she thought we were sleeping.

My chest pinches as I reach out, giving her hand a quick squeeze. "You're in luck. I keep room in the budget for pro bono procedures, and I have enough left to do one more before the end of the year."

Her jaw slackens and she stares at me, eyes suddenly brimming with tears like I just told her she won the lottery. "*You're serious?*"

"As a heart attack." I offer Guillermo my fist to bump.

He does, looking at me with a little more warmth than he was previously. Kids his age, ten or eleven, start rolling their eyes and crossing their arms when I walk into the exam room with a lab coat that's tie-dyed and adorned with buttons shaped like dancing, smiling teeth. It takes some work to win them over—they're infinitely cooler than I am, after all—but we always get there.

Victory is sweet.

Grinning more to myself than Guillermo, I stand, gesturing to the hall. "Go ahead and head up front. Lisa will get you scheduled for the extraction. I'll see you guys on Friday."

Guillermo's mom lingers in the doorway, waiting until her son is safely out of earshot before turning to me. She wipes her eyes. "Can't thank you enough, Doctor Roth. I'm not gonna lie, I didn't know how I was gonna buy groceries this week, never mind dental surgery." She hugs me, and my eyes are stinging too by the time she pulls away. "You're getting a dish of *the best* fucking chicken I cook. No arguments."

I chuckle, holding up both hands in mock surrender. "I wouldn't dare."

The moment she's gone, all the energy seems to drain out of me at once. I slump back against the supply station, pinching the bridge of my nose. I want to regret offering, because it's December and god knows my pro bono budget was gone by February, but I couldn't just let the kid walk around in pain while his mom hates herself for not being able to fix it.

I can survive the financial hit. They can't.

Tilting my head back until it hits the cabinets with a hollow *thud*, I allow myself a few seconds of exhaustion. I know what I'm doing is important. I'm helping people, *helping kids,* but the strain never seems to ease up. Every day seems to bring a new set of problems my limited resources can't solve while the state of my personal life grows grimmer.

My five-year relationship, which should be speeding toward wedding bells and diapers right about now, is instead hobbling along with the help of a trained counselor.

I can hardly blame Lindsey for being unhappy. When we met, I was about to graduate from dental school. I only had to get through one last internship at the clinic in my old neighborhood before graduating, then I would have finally been able to accept that six-figure job offer at a practice in the financial district. I was bound for a lucrative career, cementing veneers onto Wall Street bros, until my *idiot* heart got involved.

Somehow, my girlfriend found herself dating a poor, inner-city dentist. A poor, inner-city dentist who still hasn't asked her to marry him, despite the titanic-sized hints she's been dropping daily for over a year. The last time we had sex—*fuck*. I don't remember. Was it three months ago? Four? I flex my wrist at the thought, grimacing.

I'm due at couples therapy soon, where I'll spend the better part of an hour struggling to explain to myself, Lindsey, and the counselor why the thought of getting married makes me break out in hives.

Cursing under my breath, I muster what's left of my energy and push off the wall. Most of the dental assistants and hygienists have already gone home, but I get a few warm smiles and waves from the office staff as they head out into the night, bundled up in winter gear. Fighting off another wave of bitter exhaustion, I move through the quiet building, turning off lights and shutting down machinery as I go.

It's still early, but the city seems unnaturally dark as I open the front door, icy wind biting at my exposed skin. The forecasted storm is blowing in, and I pull up the collar of my coat as I fumble with the keys to the practice. I'm just turning back to the street when a prickle of awareness makes me pause, lingering in the shadowy doorway. Chills that have nothing to do with the winter air crawl up my spine as I scan the street, looking for the source of the sudden *wrongness* I'm gripped with.

There's nothing. Everything looks as it should, but even after finding nothing out of the ordinary, I don't move. It's there—the *unease*. Something isn't right. I may not be able to see it, but that doesn't make it any less true. The longer I stand here the more certain I become.

Despite being a grown man—tall, well built, and hardly an easy target—I'm not fool enough to believe I could fight off an armed gunman. A mugger wouldn't still be waiting around while his chance to get a jump on me in the shadows slips away, though. There are people making their way home down the sidewalk, and they all seem to be oblivious to whatever it is I'm sensing.

Snowflakes swirl beneath the beams of light cast by the streetlights, sparkling like millions of gold flecks in the wintery air. The beauty of the scene only heightens my paranoia, as though Mother Nature is lulling me into a false sense of security.

I shake myself. This is ridiculous. It's getting late, and I can't stay here all night, waiting for god knows what. I'll be late for the session with Lindsey if I don't leave right now, and I'm already too worn down to stomach the inevitable fight that would result.

Gritting my teeth and ignoring the uncomfortable tightening in my chest, I force myself out onto the sidewalk, still half expecting to encounter something sinister.

Nothing happens. *Of course*, nothing happens. As I turn toward my car, though, feeling ridiculous, movement in the corner of my eye makes my steps falter all over again. Whipping around to stare at the spot, my pulse races. There, tucked between several overflowing trash bins in front of the building neighboring mine... something is alive.

Cautiously, I edge close enough to the curb to see into the small space. When I finally do, I'm struck by that feeling of wrongness all over again.

There, wrapped in cheap blankets amidst the overflowing trash bins, is a teenage girl.

She can't be older than seventeen or eighteen, but what I can see of her face is too hard for such a young person. As I watch, a car drives by, spraying gray sludge over the sidewalk and the place where the girl is hiding, soaking her meager source of warmth. Still, she doesn't move.

I'm rooted to the spot, wracked with indecision. There's a major storm blowing in. Already the mayor is calling for school and business closings tomorrow. Even in bright sunshine, this is hardly the safest street in New York for a young woman alone.

Is she planning to *sleep* out here? Where the hell are her parents?

Stomach knotting, I glance at my watch. It's already late, I'm physically and emotionally exhausted, and yet I can't bring myself to turn away, head to my car and mind my own damn business. Plenty of people are passing her by, too caught up in their own struggles to worry about one more lost, hopeless soul on the sidewalk.

I can't just *leave her here*. A kid that age doesn't end up on the street if they have any other option. Wherever she came from... I can't imagine.

Ah, hell.

"Excuse me!" I call before I can talk myself out of it, stepping a little closer.

Her shoulders tense, but she doesn't turn to look at me or even acknowledge she heard my call.

Fair enough. I'm a stranger, and the adults in her life have obviously failed monumentally for her to end up here. She's brave. If I were in her place, I'd probably be sprinting in the opposite direction.

Careful to keep a respectful distance between us, I edge to the lip of the sidewalk, facing her from ten feet away. Up close, I can see the hollow of her cheeks, smudges of dirt or shadow making her look even gaunter. There's a horrible, dark bruise coloring the skin around her left eye, and a split in her lip looks barely scabbed over. Beneath the hood of her coat, the girl's dark hair is cut low to her scalp in uneven chunks, like someone hacked it away.

My stomach churns. *Holy fuck.*

It's only the fear I'll scare her that keeps me from demanding to know who did this to her. I'm not a violent man, I've never been in a fight or attacked anyone, but I find myself wishing fervently that I have the chance to make the person who did this feel even a fraction of the pain they inflicted on this girl. My hands curl into fists in my pockets.

Shifting forward into the light, I offer her a polite smile. "I'm sorry to bother you—"

"So don't." Her voice is strong, and her jaw lifts defiantly. She's still resolutely avoiding my gaze, staring blankly at the dirty sidewalk.

I let out a long breath, the vapor curling through the freezing night air as I try to decide what to do. In the five minutes since I walked outside, the temperature has dropped, and it won't be long before she's in serious trouble. "Listen," I say, adopting the reasonable, persuasive voice I reserve for my teenage patients, "I just don't want you to get killed being out here. It's going to get below freezing tonight."

If the threat of freezing to death is even remotely concerning to her, the girl doesn't show it. "I'll be fine."

Okay. Fine. We can move on to the back-up plan. My hand finds my wallet in my pocket. "There's a shelter a few blocks away. Why don't you let me give you money to take the bus over there."

She hugs her legs close to her chest as a gust of wind barrels through the tunnel of tall buildings on either side of the street, ruffling the few strands of dark hair escaping from beneath her knit cap. Still, she won't meet my eye.

"I'll pass. You offered, you did your moral duty or whatever. You can go." She sounds so strong, so sure, but of course a kid who ended up on the streets would be good at putting on a brave face. She has to be scared out of her mind—anyone would be.

What the hell am I supposed to do? I can't let her stay here, not while knowing I might return to work tomorrow morning and find her corpse frozen stiff against that trash can. There's a good chance she's still underage. If she won't go willingly, I could call protective services or the police and let them deal with her, but that plan doesn't sit right with me. She may be young, but she's not a child. If she's willing to freeze to death on the street rather than go to a shelter or home, what business do I have to send her back to whatever or whoever she's running from?

Sucking in a lungful of icy air, I make a decision. "Okay, here's what we're going to do," I say with a cheerful bravado I don't feel. "I'm a dentist. That's my practice in the building just behind you."

She doesn't reply, still staring straight ahead, but I know she can hear me.

"Inside, there's a hall that leads to all the chairs and procedure rooms. At the very end, my office is on the right. It says 'Doctor Roth' on the door, that's me. I'm going to go back in and put some blankets on the couch in there. When I leave again, I'm going to *forget* to set the code. The cleaning crew will hopefully be in at six. They're not exactly reliable, but the place will definitely be empty until then. There's a deadbolt on the front door, and my office. It's safe..."

My words trail away and I gaze at the girl's profile, hoping for some sign of acceptance or acknowledgement. After an age, something in her hardened expression seems to crack and she turns away from me, hiding her pale face in the thin, felt blanket she's wrapped in.

Okay. She heard.

Striding back inside, I do exactly as I told her I would. After disarming the security system, I flick on the lights in the hallway and grab a stack of the blankets we keep for patients in recovery. I'm halfway back to the door when it occurs to me that she's probably hungry. I don't have much to offer for food, but manage to scrounge up a few granola bars and a can of grapefruit seltzer from my desk drawer.

Nothing will make this situation okay or erase the gut-wrenching sorrow that's filled me for this stranger, but she'll be out of danger.

By the time I step back outside, the place beside the trash cans is just a shadowy patch of empty sidewalk, now. I crane my neck, trying to spot her somewhere along the snowy sidewalk, but the street is completely deserted now. She might have run off or had a friend pick her up—*Christ*, I hope she has someone who cares enough about her to make sure she doesn't sleep on the street during a snowstorm.

Still, I don't turn back to lock the door.

My car is parked around the corner. Instead of driving toward the appointment, though, I circle the block and park across the street from the practice. From here, I have a clear view of the front door and the empty stretch of sidewalk on either side of it.

Five minutes pass, then ten, and I've almost decided to go lock up when movement in the shadows makes my heart leap into my throat.

She's back.

I watch, pulse thudding, as the girl edges along the side of the building, carefully looking both ways to make sure I'm not waiting to ambush her. *Smart.* She lingers at the door for a long time, gazing at the cheerful, brightly colored logo on the glass. Finally, with one last cautious look up and down the street, she reaches for the handle and pulls it open, slipping inside.

The gnawing fear and panic inside me quiet a little, and I settle back in my seat as Christmas music plays softly on the radio. The snow is beginning to fall harder, accumulating on the hood of my car. I need to get to that appointment, but I stay where I am. It's probably beyond idiotic to let a homeless girl—a possible runaway—into my practice unattended. The narcotics are safely locked up, but there are still plenty of things she could take. I might very well come back tomorrow morning to find the place has been robbed blind.

For whatever reason, the possibility doesn't worry me as much as it should. I barely spoke to her, but that flash of emotion I glimpsed after telling her I'd leave the office open was enough.

She isn't going to steal anything.

Filled with a grim sort of satisfaction, I've just shifted the car into drive when movement from the front window catches my eye. Until seconds ago, the waiting room was concealed by drawn blinds. Now they're open, and a shadowy figure is moving around inside.

What the hell is she doing?

My question is answered almost instantly as the girl stands on the chairs lined up in front of the window, her hand moving in steady circles over the glass. I can't see her face or even what she's wearing, but the action is unmistakable.

Cleaning. She's cleaning the waiting room.

Throat tight, I lean back, watching until she draws away from the glass and the blinds fall back into place.

My phone rings and I glance down at the screen, wincing at the sight of Lindsey's name. I'm already fifteen minutes late, and it will take me another ten to get to the counselor's office.

I hit accept. "I'm sorry. I'll be there soon."

"Asher, do you know—" I'm hardly listening to her frustration, though. Reaching into my center console, I pull out a pen and a pad of paper, then begin to write.

"I'll be there soon," I repeat as soon as Lindsey breaks

for air. Before she can begin again, I hang up. Carefully folding the note, I ignore the ringing of my phone in the cupholder as I step outside and jog back across the quiet, snowy street. It only takes a few seconds to shove the paper under the door and retreat back to my car.

I'm already late and the damage is done, but I'm don't regret it. My relationship isn't more important than a girl's life. I'll explain what happened when I get there, and Lindsey will understand.

We're going to be fine.

Thank you for cleaning the office. It wasn't necessary, but I appreciate it nonetheless. As I mentioned, we've had issues with the reliability of our current cleaning crew. If you're interested in taking the job, please leave a note on my desk. In return, you can stay here as frequently as you need and I'll leave cash on my desk as payment for your time.
You have my word that you will be safe in my practice, and I will never infringe upon your privacy. As far as I'm concerned, outside business hours, this place is your home.

If you accept, the door code is 39183.
Thanks again.

-Doctor Roth

Doctor Roth,
Thank you very much for your kind offer. I accept the job and I promise I won't let you down.
-Allison

one

ADINA

PRESENT DAY

I'M EXHAUSTED, and I haven't even opened my eyes yet.

On the floor beside me, my phone chirps loudly, announcing the beginning of yet another endless day. I think (groggily) that I deserve some sort of award for not chucking it at the wall. It would feel good, a convenient way to vent some of my frustration, but I thankfully have enough self-control to keep myself from breaking something I can't afford to replace.

What is wrong with me?

I've been running on four hours of sleep for years now. It's a necessity when you're trying to cram four years of college into three, not get fired from two jobs, and perform admirably enough in an internship to lock down a solid reference. Technically, I could work less at the coffee shop and get a few more hours of rest every night. However, I did the math and the money I earn from the extra work makes up for the six—or eight—cups of coffee I have to drink throughout the day to keep my brain operational.

Unfortunately, anything *less* than four isn't an option, because shit tends to go south. Fast. I basically dissolve into a useless puddle of goo: dropping things, forgetting where I'm going, and walking into stationary objects. I still have scars from the great lamp-post collision of last summer, and I ended up having to miss an entire week of work because my boss wouldn't let me serve coffee and stale donuts with a giant scab on my forehead.

After years of trial and error, the four-hour rule has been thoroughly tried, tested, and cemented into law. *It works*, damn it, and I can't understand why it's suddenly... *not*. In this city, time is money, and I'm broke as fuck. I can't afford to sacrifice more of my day to something as unproductive as sleep, which makes my current predicament all the more stressful.

Last night, it was all I could do to finish cleaning Doctor Roth's practice before collapsing on the couch in his office, fully dressed. That was just before midnight, which means I got a full *six* hours of sleep. That's way more than enough, more than I've allowed myself in weeks, but I'm still just as bone-tired as I was yesterday.

Maybe I'm getting sick?

A familiar prickle of anxiety forces me to crack one eye, staring blearily around at the office for signs I missed something in my usual cleaning routine. Everything looks as it should, but I'll do a quick scan of the building before I leave for the day. I can't lose this job. Not just because I need the money—and having a free place to sleep is the only reason I can afford to go to college—but because the thought of letting down Doctor Roth is unbearable.

The night we met happened to be my personal rock bottom.

After an entire childhood that was, objectively, one shitty turn of events after another, I'd stopped expecting anything to go right for me. At only seventeen, I was so worn down by life that the prospect of dying alone on the cold, dark street wasn't scary. I'd *seen* scary, lived and breathed it. A quiet, anonymous death seemed like a mercy.

What did it matter if I died? Nobody knew me, nobody was looking for me, and there wasn't a single soul who would miss me if I vanished off the face of the Earth. My entire existence was just... clutter: useless, unimportant, and taking up space that could be used for someone else.

If a tree falls in a forest and there's no one there to hear it, does it make a sound? Sure, but *it doesn't matter*, and neither did I.

I don't know how long I was sitting on that sidewalk, ignored or avoided by every single person who passed me by, one more homeless teenager on the streets of New York. The tears had been dry on my cheeks for hours, and the panic gripping my chest had long since faded to the occasional, dull twinge. In fact—and I'm still not sure if it was the cold or my emotional state—I didn't feel much of anything in that moment.

I didn't know it, but for the first time in my life, I'd unwittingly ended up in exactly the right place at exactly the right time.

Doctor Roth didn't walk past me like every other person on the street that day.

He saw me.

He thought I mattered.

He gave me a chance.

At first, I thought the guy talking to me was going to

offer me cash to pee on him or something. Creeps who prey on homeless, seventeen-year-old runaways aren't exactly few and far between. I was numb, and tired, and kind of hoping I would freeze to death sooner rather than later because the whole business was pretty boring, but I wasn't concerned about handling myself. I had a five-inch steak knife in my pocket, and my hand had tightened on the handle with every word the strange guy said to me.

He *seemed* nice, but even then, I had enough experience with selfish, cruel people to know that in the beginning, they don't *seem* selfish and cruel. You can't know someone's true motives, and I was willing to bet every penny I didn't have that the guy wasn't talking to me out of the goodness of his heart.

The longer he spoke, though, the more difficult it became to keep telling myself that. His voice was kind, gentle, and endlessly patient, even while I was being a bit of an asshole.

Then, somehow, his offer managed to shatter the sense of numbness and quiet, grim acceptance that had protected me from my own feelings. All the shit I'd buried deep down, that I never wanted to think about ever again, came rushing to the surface and it was terrible. Laying on the couch in his office that first night, I allowed myself to cry for the first time in what must have been years. Huge, gut-wrenching, gasping sobs that probably sounded like I was dying. I *wasn't* dying, though. I was alive. *I was freakin' alive*, and it was kind of terrifying to realize that I wanted to stay that way.

As crazy as it sounds, one single person treating me like a human being—like my life was worth saving—was all it took for me to start hoping that things might just get better. Maybe there were people that were good. Maybe the world wasn't quite as terrible a place as it had always been to me, and maybe—*just maybe*—all that shitty luck had finally run out.

I still didn't trust him, though.

For weeks, I slept clutching the knife under my pillow and carefully waited in the shadows of the buildings across the street for him to leave every night. I signed all communication with a fake name, Allison, just in case he got curious and decided to look up Adina Collier in the state's database of missing people. Nobody was out searching for me, but child protective services would certainly swoop in and drag me back to the group home if a well-meaning dentist told them where to find me. There were only six months until my eighteenth birthday, and it was a risk I couldn't take.

It hasn't been easy, clawing my way up from rock bottom with no one to fall back on but myself, but I've done it... Well, I've *kind of* done it. In a haphazard, sleep-deprived, no-idea-what-I'm-doing kind of way.

Let's call it a work in progress.

My life still seems to hang in perpetual limbo between homelessness and stability, swinging one way or the other depending on how many hours I manage to snag at the coffee shop. It's always in the back of my mind that I'm one lost job or unexpected medical bill away from the life I've built like a deck of cards falling down around me. Even with all that, though, I'm so much luckier than some people in my situation. I got my GED, I'm in college, and I have two jobs and a safe place to sleep.

If I disappeared, people would notice.

Doctor Roth would notice.

My heart performs its usual flip-flop at the thought of my boss, and I roll to the edge of the couch, feeling blindly for the little slip of paper I found waiting for me last night.

We've been doing this for years, passing little letters back and forth, ever since that first offer he slipped under the door about taking over cleaning the practice. Some of them are all business, me telling him the office manager forgot to order more toilet paper or that the radiator in exam room three is doing that weird clanking noise again. Other times, he asks me about college or I tell him jokes.

We're friends, if you can call two people friends who've only met once and now communicate exclusively via sticky notes.

It's pretty ridiculous to be this attracted to a man I've only seen properly on a dentist office website, who calls me by the wrong name (though this is, admittedly, my fault), and is probably twice my age, but I can't help it. My feelings for Asher Roth have grown steadily over the years, beginning as admiration and gratitude, and took an *adult* turn somewhere along the way.

My first impression of Doctor Roth couldn't have been further from the truth. On top of everything he's done for me, this whole practice is littered with evidence of what a good person he is: thank-you notes from grateful parents and clumsy crayon drawings of the dentist with—judging by the names on the employee lockers—the same loyal staff working for him as when I started cleaning the practice three years ago.

Groaning quietly, I give myself a silent pep talk—and proper shaming—to get my butt up. Difficulty with this is a common side effect of the four-hour rule, and all the practice I've had doesn't make it any easier to force my body into a sitting position.

Sunlight is just beginning to filter in through the small,

narrow window that runs along the top of the wall behind Doctor Roth's desk, illuminating the familiar room in all its glory—faded linoleum, generic art, and all. The most colorful aspect of the whole room is the wall to my right. It's bedecked with what must be hundreds of thank-you notes, Christmas cards, and drawings that range from crayon scribbles to carefully shaded pencil masterpieces on torn binder paper.

My eyes catch on one of a tall, mostly anatomically correct person wearing glasses and a technicolor lab coat, and I feel the corners of my lips twitch as I get to my feet.

In the corner of the office, there's a closet where Doctor Roth lets me keep a plastic storage bin filled with my things. Inside the closet, I see the familiar assortment of scrubs and about a dozen lab coats that were obviously designed to make his patients laugh. Some of them have silly buttons, and one is made of leopard print and trimmed in pink fur. Last year for Christmas, I went to the craft store and got a huge bag of multicolored rhinestones. I spent the better part of a weekend sewing them onto the collar and into the shape of a tooth on the front pocket.

He wears it more than any of the others, and it makes warmth expand inside me every time I spot it back from the cleaners.

The men I grew up around were always so dedicated to appearing tough or masculine. They wouldn't be caught dead wearing a sparkling coat to make a child more comfortable at a scary dentist's office, but Doctor Roth is nothing like them.

My back-up alarm chimes threateningly and I dress quickly, darting to the employee bathroom to brush my teeth and run my fingers through my hair. I've been cleaning the office long enough that I must have been moving on autopilot last night, because everything is clean despite my level of exhaustion.

Confident that my job is done, I carefully fold my blankets back into the bin and grab my backpack, doing a quick sweep over the office to make sure I've left no trace of my presence here. I know Doctor Roth would never throw me out for leaving a dirty sock on the floor, but that splinter of fear has buried so far inside me, I doubt I could ever dig it out.

I may technically be a squatter, but this is the safest, happiest place I've ever lived. Nobody has ever hurt me here, and the anxiety I feel about the circumstances is entirely self-inflicted. It's *my home*, but as I head toward the front door, the familiar, sick swoop of fear makes my pace falter. I pause with my hand outstretched, fingers resting on the cool, metal deadbolt. I know better than anyone how fast things can go from good to a total shitstorm, and every day a little part of me wants to run right back to the safety of Doctor Roth's couch.

Defiantly, I stare through the glass and suck in a long, slow breath.

Letting my past make me afraid and cowering away from the world is easy. Going out there with my head held high, fighting tooth and nail for the life I want, is hard. I'm not a coward, and I'm not afraid of working my ass off.

Not wasting another second, I turn the lock and step outside.

Allison,

Don't think I haven't noticed you're avoiding the question. <u>Do. You. Need. Extra. Money. For. Books?</u> I'll keep pestering you until I get a straight answer. Seriously, though, I'm happy to help. I know you won't take money for nothing, but I've been meaning to get the restrooms painted... If I got the supplies, I could pay you extra to take care of it for me?

Deal?

Okay, great. Paint will be waiting for you next weekend. Also, I need your expertise on this joke I've been workshopping for the patients. On a scale from 1 to 10 (1 being the lamest, 10 being ultra, incredibly cool), where am I sitting?

<u>What did the dentist say to a golfer with a cavity?</u>

<u>You have a hole in one!</u>

Sincerely,
The pain-in-the-ass dentist who cares about your education.

Dear Pain-in-the-Ass Dentist who Cares About my Education,

Firstly, I greatly approve of the name change. Super appropriate.

Secondly, everything is UNDER CONTROL with school. I swear. My second job is pretty much taking care of all the out-of-pocket expenses that financial aid doesn't cover. Still, I'd be happy to paint the bathrooms. No need to pay me extra; it's the least I can do.

Thirdly, do not tell anyone that joke. No kid under the age of eight knows anything about golf, and you will be mocked by anyone older. I'm doing you a favor here. It's a 2 out of 10.

Sincerely, The richest college student ever

I MET Ruby Johnson three years ago during freshman orientation.

Everyone else seemed to be worried about finding friends and scoping out the best parties, but I had other things on my mind. The home healthcare job I'd snagged had fallen through, and I was frantically trying to find something else in order to pay for books and other supplies I'd need for my first ever semester of college.

All the social-work majors had been invited to attend a mixer with the faculty at one of the activity rooms in the student center. While I had no particular desire to *"mixer"* with anyone, I'd gone to suck up to my future professors, and regretted it almost immediately.

Nobody else seemed to have a problem talking to people they'd never met. They all wore the right things and *didn't* hover beside the snack tray like a hungry raccoon. If they were worried they'd say something wrong or that someone would notice they didn't belong here, none of them showed it. Dressed in their best blazers, my future classmates were prepared to charm our professors—the future reference givers—with wholesome anecdotes about why they chose social work as a major.

Meanwhile, I lingered at the edge of the room wishing I'd worn something, *anything*, nicer than jeans, a T-shirt, and beat-up flip-flops.

Over and over again, I tried to convince myself to go talk to someone. College was step one in my grand ambition of living a normal, reasonably happy life, so shouldn't I be attempting to be normal and reasonably happy? I must have come up with a dozen charming and self-deprecating ways to laugh off my fashion faux pas, because surely it wasn't even *that* big of a deal. Shit happens, right?

Over and over again, I lost my nerve.

In retrospect, I can hardly blame my former self for being anxious. After all, at that point I had eighteen years of experience in being the dirty, weird-smelling kid in stained clothes who sometimes wouldn't show up to school for weeks at a time. Then, I was the teenager who wrote on the bathroom walls and talked back to teachers. After that, I was the foster kid parents told their kids to be nice to, but never wanted them to hang out with. Hated. Pitied. *Other*.

My life had changed, but did that really matter? Surely anyone who looked my way would be able to see me for what I was.

Ruby seemed to appear out of nowhere, offering a pained, commiserating smile that I didn't return. Tall, blonde, and perfect, she reminded me of a Barbie doll in ripped black jeans and a death metal T-shirt. Apparently oblivious to my internal spiral, she proceeded to matter-of-factly tell me every single detail of her life story in between bites of cheese and pepperoni from the tray beside us. Her childhood had been almost as shitty as my own, and she'd decided to change the system from the inside. Or, if that didn't work, she was going to marry rich and spend her days designing lip rings.

Friendship requires you to open up, to offer up a little bit of yourself, but I couldn't quite do it, and Ruby didn't push.

We aren't friends, exactly. We study together sometimes, and work together for group projects. Once or twice we've eaten lunch together, but that's it. Ruby doesn't have a problem with talking about her trauma or owning up to her less than ideal life choices. I certainly don't think any less of her knowing any of it, but I can't seem to extend that same compassion to myself. After three years, she knows not to ask too many questions.

We're allies, united as outsiders, and it's better that way.

I do my best not to think about where I came from, but when I have no choice, it's easy to tell myself that everything happened *then*. This is *now*. I can't change any of it, so what's the point in dwelling on it?

Am I in denial? Absolutely, but it's working just fine for now, and there are barely enough hours in the day to sleep. When would I have time to address whatever emotional trauma was inflicted on me in my first few decades of life? I have enough on my plate.

For one thing, there's a test in my ethics seminar that I've barely studied for. Thankfully, Ruby is in the class and doesn't object to spending the morning in the library together.

She's already there when I arrive, her long, blonde hair pulled up in a messy bun, blue-light glasses resting on the bridge of her nose as she glares down at her computer screen. As I set my things on the table and smile at her, a few of the frat guys at the table to our right shoot her appreciative, hopeful glances that go utterly ignored. I can't blame them; she's ridiculously gorgeous.

Unfortunately for her admirers, however, Ruby Johnson would suck their souls out of their noses with a curly straw if they worked up the courage to talk to her. Wildly beautiful and intelligent, she might be. Tolerant of unsolicited interest, she is not.

"Hey—Oh! Thank you!" I shoot her an appreciative smile when she pushes a cup of coffee across the table toward me. My thanks gets about as much attention as the frat guys did. Ruby hums, not breaking the stare-off with her computer.

"This is such bullcrap," she mutters furiously, eyebrows pinching. "Have you ever had Professor Meadows? This stupid ho-bag gave me *a fucking C* on my paper just because I pointed out that her grading criteria is outdated as fuck."

Having known Ruby for as long as I have, I'm fairly confident that this constructive criticism for her professor wasn't given in anything resembling a respectful manner. "That sucks," I offer diplomatically, pulling out my battered laptop and charger. "I haven't had her."

Ruby huffs, snapping her computer shut and turning her attention to me. "Listen, I need a favor." She leans toward me over the table and, as suddenly as if she's flipped a switch, her voice becomes sweet, her eyes wide and imploring.

I'm instantly on alert. Those three years of experience with Ruby Johnson have also taught me that whatever it is she wants will likely be something unpleasant for me. She doesn't ask for favors very often, but when she does...

Without waiting to hear the pitch, I turn my attention to powering on my computer. "No."

"Seriously? You don't even want to hear it? Spoiler alert,

it *pays well.*" She sings the last two words, and I *hate* that they are all it takes for her to have my complete, undivided attention.

Still, I give myself a few more seconds of staring blankly at my start-up screen—because I do have some pride—before abandoning all pretense. "Fine. Let me hear it."

To her credit, Ruby doesn't point out how easily I surrender my morals when a few dollars are waved in my face. She knows what it's like, just like how I know that I can afford to have dignity once I graduate and get a good job. Until then, if I can make it through the week without overdrawing my bank account or eating something more nutritious than instant noodles, I'll call it a win.

"So you know that guy I've been seeing? Liam?"

'Seeing' seems like a bit of a stretch when she'd dump him like a hot potato if he stopped buying her designer handbags. I pause, not liking where this is going. "Uh, yeah. Sure."

No matter how broke I've gotten, I could never stomach jumping on the sugar-baby bandwagon that Ruby swears by. I don't judge her; she's doing what she has to do, and doing it well. If I'm honest with myself, I *wish* I could do the same. Sitting across from a rich guy and pretending to be interested in what he's saying sounds a hell of a lot better than handing out donuts and coffee for minimum wage night after night, then dragging my aching feet across town to Doctor Roth's practice to clean until I pass out on his office couch.

For most of my life, I was completely at the mercy of the people around me, and it didn't exactly go well. I can't stand the idea of being dependent on anyone or giving them that kind of power over me. Even trading cleaning for a place to sleep eats at me. My life may be shitty and hard, but it's *mine*. The thought of relying on a man who only wants me for my face or body... I just can't.

Ruby glances around to make sure there's no one within hearing distance, then leans in and whispers conspiratorially, "So, we were supposed to see each other tonight, but I guess he's entertaining an old friend for the weekend. He asked if I knew someone who could come with me. A double date. We'd be having drinks at the lounge in his hotel, then going to that fancy new steakhouse downtown where they put shaved gold on the porterhouse. It would be *just* dinner and drinks, Adina. I swear."

My lungs empty, and I stare blankly at the cracked screen of my laptop, reeling. "Even if I wanted to, I don't have anything to wear to a restaurant that serves golden meat, Ruby." Everything I own can fit in the bin Doctor Roth keeps for me in his office closet. I have a few office-appropriate outfits for my internship, but I wouldn't be able to get them until after the practice closes for the day.

Reaching into her backpack, Ruby whips out a black credit card and brandishes it in my face. "Liam told me to go shopping and take you along! Girl, he is so fucking rich, I don't think he even checks the statement before paying it. Want a car?"

"I'll pass." I swat her hand away, my chest growing tight. *Am I really considering this?* In my experience, if something seems too good to be true, it almost certainly is. "So he wants to pay me just to be a date for his friend?" I clarify, hating how chicken-shit I sound right now.

"That's it," Ruby insists as she tucks Liam's credit card away. "I guess the guy just went through a bad breakup or something and he feels bad for him."

I'm tempted.

Really tempted.

This wouldn't be my *job*, after all. It would just be a one-time thing, and with my internship starting next week, I know I'll have to take less hours at the coffee shop. Also, *I'm tired*. The kind of tiredness that comes from working your ass off for years without a single break. Would it be so wrong to take a shortcut? Just this once?

I swallow. "How much would it pay?"

Obviously pleased I asked, Ruby's lips curl into a smirk. "Liam said to offer a thousand. Though I bet if I tell him you're not so sure, he'd double it. The guy owns one of the fanciest hotels in the city, so he can afford it." She winks at me. "I totally talked you up, telling him how smart and pretty you are, and that you're going to be a social worker and have a heart of gold. All the good stuff."

It's like all the air has been sucked out of my lungs.

Ruby picks up her phone, and I watch her thumbs fly over the screen as my mind races just as quickly.

A *thousand* dollars for only a few hours? It would normally take me weeks to make that kind of money. With my internship, soon things will get even tighter. *I need money.*

It would be stupid not to do this, right? I mean, I wouldn't need to take my clothes off or let some guy take pictures of my feet. I'd just need to wear a new dress and make conversation with a lonely guy so his friend can slobber all over my friend. We'd be in a public place, so the risk of being murdered seems minimal, and I don't have plans until my double shift at the coffee shop tomorrow. I'm supposed to be painting the bathrooms for Doctor Roth this weekend, but if I stay up late after my double shift—

"Oh, shit." Ruby giggles, thrusting her phone in my face.

> Ruby: Hey, handsome. I don't know if my friend is game for tonight. She's SO CUTE and doesn't want to let down her boss on such short notice! 🫣

> Daddy Liam 👺🗡️: Offer her $3k to sweeten the deal, babydoll. She sounds like exactly what my friend needs.

I almost choke on my tongue. *Three thousand dollars?*

Ruby stares at me expectantly and, with all reasonable objections forgotten, I nod.

Three thousand dollars is enough to cover the lost income from all the time I'll be spending at my internship while still having plenty left over to start saving for an apartment.

I feel a not-so-little pang at the thought of never finding another note from Doctor Roth, but I've already been there too long. He's been so kind to keep this arrangement going, but I don't want to push it too far. Not to mention, it would be nice to sleep somewhere without the anxiety of what will happen to me if he suddenly decides he's had enough of our agreement.

I'll miss him, but I know it's time. All it will take is abandoning my stubborn self-reliance for a few hours.

Besides, this is my last semester. Against all odds, I've reached the final sprint of my college career. I only have a few more months of classes, internship hours, and working two jobs before I graduate and can get a job doing something that's actually meaningful.

A familiar fantasy blooms in my imagination, the one where I'm older, more beautiful and more sophisticated. I go back to the practice to thank Doctor Roth for everything he did for me, then maybe he would ask me to dinner to talk, and that would be the beginning. I know he's older than me, and more successful, but maybe if we met when I *wasn't* a homeless twenty-one-year-old sleeping on his couch...

"It'll be fun," Ruby promises as she thumbs out a message, presumably relaying the good news to her sugar daddy. "We can go shopping after the test and find you something killer to wear."

"Okay," I agree numbly, my hand pressing over the sudden point of pain in the center of my chest. It's ridiculous to feel like you're betraying a man you've only met in person once and who has never expressed even the slightest romantic interest in you.

It's just dinner. *I can do this.*

THE WITT HOTEL is one of those everlasting testaments to New York City. It's not the most polished or modern building; the marble exterior is grungy, and the doormen wear the same forest-green uniforms as they did a century ago when The Witt first opened its doors. Despite all that, the place is a mecca for old-money travelers, reliably drawing the kind of clientele who want to make a statement without standing out.

In other words, not me.

If it weren't for a comical twist of fate that landed the scholarship student in a college dorm with the heir to The Witt Hotel dynasty when we were eighteen, I would never have stepped foot in this place. Liam Witt and I were an odd pair back in the day, and we still are now. We have practically nothing in common and most of the time he drives me insane, yet he's been my closest friend for over twenty years.

Anyone would think I'd have grown accustomed to his hedonistic behavior by now, but the asshole still manages to surprise me.

"I thought you'd be pleased!" Liam's laugh draws the curious eyes of the other guests seated around us in The Witt's lounge. Being here, with him, always makes me feel like I'm in a fishbowl. People are always looking, eager to walk away from their stay with some anecdote about the hotel's infamous owner.

When Liam called me earlier this week with the invitation to spend the weekend, it seemed appealing. The practice is normally open on Saturday mornings and I typically go in Sunday to finish up paperwork, but the wedding of one of my hygienists has sent most of my staff out of town. A few days downtown on Liam's dime, catching up with my old friend, would be fun. At least, it would be better than hiding away in my godawful apartment or going to a wedding where I'd know no one but my staff.

I should have known better.

Gritting my teeth, I glare across the low lounge table at him, willing my voice to remain even. "I'm *not* pleased."

Swirling a glass of scotch that probably costs more than my car, Liam leans back in his chair, surveying me with his trademark, maddening smirk. "I thought you wanted to start dating again."

Telling this man *anything* is such a mistake. He's proven it time and again, yet I never learn.

Am I an idiot? I might be an idiot.

Setting my drink down on the antique side table to my right, I lean forward, dropping my voice so we're not overheard. "I said I want to start dating again after you got me drunk on four glasses of vintage whiskey. In what world do you take that as an invitation to *pay* a young woman to pretend to be interested in me?" A sour taste fills my mouth at the thought of it.

I have years of experience with the kind of women Liam

"dates." Attractive, charming, and obscenely wealthy, the man has a line of women enthusiastically throwing themselves at him on a daily basis. For reasons I'll never understand, though, he prefers to hire his girlfriends.

Liam lets out a heavy sigh, gazing at me pityingly. "See, *that's* how I know you need this. You're forty, not sixty-five, Asher. No single, successful, forty-year-old man refers to a hot-as-fuck college girl as a *young woman*."

Calling myself successful seems like a stretch. My practice gives away more procedures than it bills, and the distinction of *Doctor* that I'm legally allowed to tack on in front of my name is the most prestigious thing about me. I would make more money going to work for quite literally any dental clinic in the city, but I can't bring myself to do it.

Christ. I really am an idiot.

"Liam," I plead, suddenly nauseous. "Call it off."

He stares at me in silence for a long moment, apparently considering. Then, unaffected and unmoved by my panic, cheerfully shakes his head. "Request denied. This will be *good* for you, Asher. Do you know why I do the sugar daddy thing?" He lifts his eyebrows expectantly, but I barely have time to open my mouth—intending to cite his emotional immaturity—before the smug fuck is answering his own question. "Because it's *honest.* I know she's in it for the paycheck, and she knows I'm in it to have the benefits of a relationship without having to be in one. It's a business transaction. We have a grand time together while it lasts, then go our separate ways without a fuss. I think that sort of *arrangement* would be very beneficial for you right now."

My mouth has gone dry, but I manage to choke out a halfhearted retort to this speech. "You need therapy."

Liam's eyes gleam with amusement, obnoxiously satisfied with himself for rattling me. "Probably. I have sex *regu-*

larly, though. Good sex, too. Not missionary in the dark while one of you looks at your phone. Can you say the same?"

I wish fervently I could get away with lying about this, but I know I can't. Through the various ups and downs of my relationship with Lindsey, good sex wasn't exactly on the menu with any kind of reliability. Our final years included a few halfhearted attempts at "spicing it up," but nothing stuck.

My non-answer says it all.

Despite any drunken ramblings to Liam about my desire to get back out there, I haven't so much as downloaded a dating app. It just feels... *wrong*. The issues in my former relationship were almost exclusively my own fault: *my* fear of commitment, *my* preoccupation with work, *my* poor communication skills. It seems wrong to keep dating, and to put some poor, innocent woman through the ringer of my emotional immaturity, when I'm fully aware I have no business doing so.

Unattached sex is my only realistic option, but at forty years old and fresh out of a nearly seven-year relationship, I have no idea how I would orchestrate such a thing.

Liam's bright-blue eyes search my face, his carefree smirk fading at whatever he sees there. "You need to rip off the Band-Aid. Think of tonight as... practice. She's a friend of Ruby's. No need to get your panties in a twist, Asher. It's just dinner. I'm not paying her to fuck you. I mean, *I could*."

My temples throb painfully. How the hell do I get out of this? He's trying to be a good friend in his own emotionally stunted way. I appreciate the effort; however, there's quite literally nothing I'd rather do less than make stilted conversation with whatever friend his latest pseudo-girlfriend drummed up to be my date tonight.

I attempt a self-deprecating smile. "I appreciate what you're trying to do, but..." The words trail away as I glance across the lounge to gather my thoughts, and my gaze catches on a woman just stepping into the room through the polished wood doors.

Just like that, every excuse and justification I had for not being here is wiped from my brain.

I can't think, and I'm not even sure that I'm breathing, because this woman... Stunning doesn't even begin to cover it.

I'm entranced.

She can't possibly be older than her early twenties, at least a decade too young for me to be interested in, yet my conscience is nowhere to be found. I can't stop staring, my eyes roaming greedily over her, desperate to gather every detail. She's curvy, a tiny waist flowing out into round hips, her hourglass figure emphasized by the silky black dress she's wearing. Rich-brown hair tumbles in loose curls around her shoulders, and under the tasteful, dim lighting, her ivory skin seems to glow.

The most striking thing of all, though, is her beautiful, heart-shaped face. As I watch, she turns slightly toward us, taking in the room through wide eyes.

She's nervous.

I can see it in the way she's standing, with her shoulders bunched up and hands clasped tightly in front of her, like she's trying to make herself as small as possible. As I stare, a couple enters the lounge behind her and she practically jumps out of the way to let them pass. In a room full of blue-blood debutantes who move through the world like they belong, this stranger is more captivating than any of them, and she wants to fade into the walls.

We have something in common, then. Neither of us belong here.

Cupid's bow lips part, and I realize there's a woman standing beside her, leaning in close to hear what my mystery woman is saying. Her friend could be equally stunning, but for all the notice I take of her, she may as well be one of the bar stools.

Whoever this woman is... Just looking at her feels like I've stepped outside and found bright sunshine instead of snow. My whole body is heated, on edge, and humming with excitement. Every last reason I had for wanting to leave this hotel is gone, and now all I can think about is how badly I want—*need*—to talk to her.

Liam rises, lifting a hand to attract the attention of someone, and smirks over his shoulder at me. "Staying, then?"

I blink dazedly up at him. "I..." But my words are lost all over again when the two women turn toward us. I'm dimly aware of the tall blonde waving cheerfully at my friend. As befuddled and lust-drunk as I am, it takes me a moment to process the situation.

Then it hits me.

That's the woman he arranged to be my date for the evening? *Her?*

I don't have time to panic. The tall blonde whom Liam waved to is winding her way through the tables, looking very much at home amidst the well-dressed diners while her dark-haired friend follows, a deer in headlights by comparison. I see a few men turning their heads to watch the two women pass and, possessed by an illogical, territorial instinct, I stand too.

"Ruby." Liam kisses the blonde's cheek as she stops at his side, her hand curling familiarly over his arm. "Glad you could make it." Ruby preens as he leans back, looking her up and down in unabashed approval.

"This is my friend, Adina." She gestures to the brunette, and my pulse throbs as she shyly lifts her eyes to meet mine.

Adina.

I've never met anyone named that, but it suits her. Mysterious, feminine, and lovely beyond measure.

Liam gestures to me. "Wonderful to meet you at last, Adina. Ruby's told me lots of wonderful things. This is a friend of mine from my undergraduate days, Asher Roth. I promised to show him all the wonders of The Big Apple while he's in town." Turning on the pretense of pouring the girls each a glass of wine from the bottle on the table, he winks at me, and I'm too hazy with shock to understand what he's doing until it's too late.

Liam is giving me the way out he thinks I want, ensuring a no-pressure, no-strings-attached evening for me with Adina.

So quickly I'm not sure if I imagined it, her eyes drop down my body and back up to meet mine. She looks… shocked.

I swallow thickly as I take one of the glasses Liam filled and step around the table to pass it to Adina. Our fingers barely brush, but the contact is enough to send electricity surging up my arm to spread through my chest, putting every nerve in my body on alert. I'm staring, but I can't help it. *Fuck,* she's so beautiful. I've never had this kind of reaction to a woman in my life. I should correct Liam, it's not too late—

"It's nice to meet you," Adina offers, so softly it's difficult to hear her words over the neighboring tables, and her lips lift into a shy smile.

"And you." I gesture to the club chair behind her and she sits immediately, crossing her ankles beneath it gracefully.

Across from us, Ruby giggles, smacking Liam's chest playfully as he whispers something in her ear I'm positive I don't want to hear. Extracting herself from his hold, Ruby settles herself down beside her friend and regards me with a flirty, playful smirk. "So, what do you *do*, Ash? Liam's told me absolutely nothing about you." She takes her own glass from the table, casting yet another heated look toward my friend.

Tall, blonde, and thin, I can understand why Liam is attracted to her, but Ruby's beauty doesn't hit me like a goddamn truck the way Adina's does.

Hazily, I attempt to think of a single childhood crush, former girlfriend, or international celebrity I would rather be sitting with right now. I come up blank.

Christ.

"Asher is in business. He owns a *very* successful chain of healthcare facilities," Liam tells her, his confidence in the lie not faltering for a second, and my stomach churns. I don't know how men do this—boast about themselves or make up lies to impress women. I'm not even the one saying this shit and it's unbearable. Adina isn't impressed either. On the contrary, she seems to shrink in on herself at his words, shying away from my gaze as if I might find her wanting.

Ha. The poor thing has a better chance of me throwing her over my shoulder, taking her upstairs to my room, and eating her pussy against the massive glass windows until she's too swollen and sensitive to take anymore.

I've never considered myself much of an exhibitionist,

but I know if this angel allowed me between those thighs, I'd want the whole city to know it.

Ruby leans forward, and her bright-red lips curl into a practiced smile. "*Very* impressive, Mr. Roth. I had no idea Liam has such impressive friends."

"I—" My words falter and I clear my throat, taken aback by the possessive instincts coming to life inside me. This is the moment where I would halfheartedly make a joke about how Liam is attempting to make me sound more important than I really am and tell her the truth... That I'm an aggressively middle-class dentist. But, *fuck*, if even my closest friend thinks that my real life isn't noteworthy, neither will Adina.

I'm so far out of my league it's fairly ridiculous. Not only is she the sexiest woman I've ever seen, and half my age, but apparently her financial situation leads her to date rich men for money. Regardless of my wild attraction to her, this isn't going to *go* anywhere.

My moment of paralysis is long enough for Ruby and Liam to lose interest in us, his hand finding her thigh as he leans over to murmur something undoubtedly filthy in her ear. I wince, turning my gaze desperately back to Adina, and I start with surprise when I find her looking at me.

This close, I can see her eyes are green and flecked with gold, so vibrant they stand out even in the dim light of The Witt's lounge. She's nibbling nervously on her bottom lip, and her cheeks go pink when I catch her looking, but she doesn't turn away.

Something seems to loosen inside me.

"I'm sorry. About..." I tilt my head subtly toward our two unbearable friends, grimacing.

"We'll hopefully survive the secondhand embarrassment," Adina replies with a wry little smile, lifting her glass to her lips.

I chuckle, finding that I'm relaxed enough to manage a sip of my own drink. The restaurant is lit by clusters of antique lanterns hung over every table. They cast warm beams of light throughout the room, bright enough to see what you're doing, but low enough to create an intimate, seductive atmosphere.

A minute ticks by, then two. Adina and I sneak looks at each other while Liam and Ruby become lost in their own world. I may not have been on a date in years, but I better figure it out fast. All thoughts of leaving evaporated the moment she walked into the room, and now I find myself desperately wondering how I can make the night last longer.

Talking to her would be a good start.

I clear my throat. "Tell me about yourself, Adina." The moment I've spoken the words, I wish I could take them back. Never has anyone offered a more generic, unimaginative conversation starter. For fuck's sake, I'm pretty sure I asked Rob, the dental assistant I hired last year, the same thing at the start of his job interview.

Adina peers over at me, one corner of her lips lifting shyly. "I'm not very exciting."

I doubt that. I'm more excited than I've ever been in my life, and she's spoken all of three sentences to me. I smile encouragingly, shifting so I'm facing her. "Do you work?"

"I'm a student," she responds gently, playing with the stem of her glass. "I also work at a coffee shop and have a cleaning gig."

In college and working two jobs? "Impressive."

Her nose wrinkles, and I think it's the most adorable thing I've ever seen. "If you say so."

"I do." I set my drink on the table, giving her my full attention. "I did the same while I was in school. So it would really help my ego if you'd accept the compliment." Those green eyes meet mine, and the musical little giggle that falls from her lips makes me feel about ten feet tall.

"In that case, compliment accepted. What did you do? Your college jobs, I mean."

"Mopped floors at a retirement home and worked in the school cafeteria. I went to class smelling like grilled cheese and mop water."

I only have to hear it once for Adina's laugh to become my favorite noise in the world. It's... free. She isn't humoring me or trying to get attention, but eyes from the surrounding tables flick over to her anyway, some disapproving, others envious.

Adina doesn't seem to notice any of them, though, because she hasn't stopped looking at me.

"It worked out for you." She smiles slyly, her eyes still sparkling. "Though you chose a more profitable career path than I'm planning to, so I'll reserve judgment."

"What are you studying?" I ask, taken off guard by how eager I am to piece together who this woman is. I could ask her questions all night and still have more.

"Social work. With a concentration in child development and welfare." She sips her wine, and I'm not sure if it's the light or my imagination, but I swear I see the tiniest shadow cross her stunning face.

For a moment, I consider telling her what I really do, because I *want* her to know.

It's a fleeting impulse, though, and one I quickly dismiss. She isn't interested in me. Liam paid her for her time, likely hoping to keep me occupied while he enjoys her friend. A quick glance toward the couple entwined across from us confirms my suspicions. I'm attracted to her. It would be stupid to pretend otherwise when my cock has been throbbing viciously against my fly since we sat down, but this isn't a date. Not a real one.

At the end of the night, she's going to go back to her life, and I'm going to go back to mine. There will be no texting or calling, no second date, and certainly no third. Adina, if that's even her real name, is an actress. She's putting on a show, and apparently I'm just desperate enough to lap it up. Disgusted with myself, I turn my eyes to the room around us, ignoring the weight of her eyes on me.

"So did you study business or..." Her voice trails away, tentative, unsure, and *genuine*.

Shit. Unable to help myself, I turn, and my heart wrenches at the sight of the worried little crease between her brows. I'm being cold, giving this poor woman whiplash, and *I wish I didn't care*. This whole situation is so messed up—

"I'm *starving*." Ruby moans, drawing all eyes to her.

Liam nods obligingly, lifting a hand to signal the hostess. "Let's all go have dinner down the street at the Claremont. I'm bored of the food here. I'll have to speak to the chef."

"No." Suddenly, all eyes are on me, and I still. Embarrassment tightens in my chest, and I have no idea what I'm going to say. The whole plan for tonight was to have drinks, then dinner, but now all I want is to steal Adina away from Liam and Ruby. She might not want that, might prefer to have dinner and not be alone with me, but there's no way to check now. All I can do is offer, and try to give her an easy out.

Gathering my courage, I look to Adina. "Why don't we

let them go ahead? I'd love to continue our discussion. If you're not hungry, that is."

I've barely finished speaking before she's nodding her agreement.

"I'm really not. I'm sorry, Ruby. Is that alright?" She smiles apologetically at her friend, but Ruby is clearly pleased with this turn of events.

"Of course." She beams, wrapping one perfectly manicured hand around Liam's arm as they stand, looking down at us with matching expressions of amusement. "Have fun, you two."

ADINA

THIS ISN'T how I thought tonight would go.

I was anxious all afternoon leading up to this, barely able to enjoy the spa day Ruby treated us to or the new clothes she insisted on purchasing me "for options." I can only assume *Daddy Liam*'s credit card saw significant abuse, because I spent hours being waxed, tweezed, exfoliated, and made up. I barely recognized the woman in the mirror when we were done. Unfortunately, while I'm pretty sure I look better than I ever have in my life on the outside, I'm a certified hot mess internally.

Or, I *was* a hot mess, until I caught sight of the man I am supposed to be pretending to be attracted to.

Yeah... Pretending is not necessary.

I don't know what I expected, but coming face-to-face with Doctor Asher Roth was definitely not it.

I'm pretty proud of myself for not passing out on the spot. I mean, *what are the chances?* There have to be millions of men in this city, and I end up sitting beside the one I've been trying to convince myself I'm not in love with for the better part of three years.

At first I thought it had to be some weird, exhaustion-induced hallucination. The only time I've ever seen his face, apart from the night we met, has been during some light internet stalking. There's a picture of him on the practice's website, grinning at the camera with his bright-blue eyes standing out brilliantly against the white background. I knew he was handsome, obviously, but I had no way of knowing that a professional headshot *does not* do Asher Roth justice.

His hair is more gray than light brown, and the wire-framed glasses balanced on his nose are too big to be considered fashionable. Even the clothes he's wearing, from his vest and bow tie down to the scuffed dress shoes, are buttoned up and practical. If I didn't know better, I'd have put him down as a high school chemistry teacher or the owner of a bookshop. He's... nerdy. And it's adorable.

Is adorable the right word?

Probably not, considering the things I'm feeling for him are *aggressively* non-platonic.

Holy crap. I can't believe this is actually happening.

For as long as I can remember, I've carefully keep a ten-foot concrete wall planted between myself and any kind of romantic relationship.

I have enough self-awareness to know that the constant, hollow yearning I have to be loved is the most dangerous thing about myself. It doesn't take a therapist to figure out why, either, or to know what might happen to me if I ever let myself forget it: The damaged, forgotten girl who was overlooked and tossed through her childhood like a lost toy grows up and clings to stability wherever she can get it... Even if it's toxic. Even if it's abusive. Even if it's the opposite of everything she's ever wanted.

I won't let that happen. There's no safe place for me to

land if my life goes belly up. Letting someone in would be tantamount to handing over my entire future on a silver platter and blindly trusting them to take care of it. Right now, falling in love isn't a risk I can take.

Having a crush on the one man on the planet that I *do* trust, my kind, handsome boss—who happens to be so wildly out of my league it isn't even funny and thinks my name is Allison—was safe. He's a dentist, an actual professional who owns his own business and has his crap together. Meanwhile, I'm struggling just to keep my head above water and not drop dead of exhaustion and/or caffeine overconsumption.

Asher was never going to catch feelings for me, so what did it matter if I pined away from a distance?

All those daydreams I've had about meeting him—they were so far down the road. I wanted us to be equals. I wanted to actually stand a chance with him. Never in a million years would I have expected him to be interested in me right now, and even in my wildest dreams, I never thought my attraction to him would be so intense.

It's too soon. I'm not ready for this.

Asher Roth has had a piece of my heart for three years, a piece that's seemed to get bigger with every messy note I found waiting for me on his desk. What would he say if he knew the beautiful, elegantly dressed woman beside him was the same girl he practically pulled out of the trash three years ago?

Would he still want to pretend he's only here for the weekend?

Would he be horrified?

Would he be stunned by the incredible coincidence that threw us together not just once, but twice?

I feel like I'm being torn apart, but walking away isn't

an option. From the moment I spotted him across the room, it's like my heart has been attached to a string and the other end is tied to Asher Roth. I can feel it, tugging gently whenever I try to shy away from him or pretend I'm absorbed in the contents of my wine glass. Even if he only wants me for the night, even if this ruins whatever flimsy hopes I had for *someday*... I can't leave.

Peeking over my wine glass, I gaze at the beautiful man sitting beside me. Every time he reaches for his drink, revealing a few more inches of lean, muscular forearm, my thighs press a little tighter together. Whenever he leans slightly toward me, his button-up shirt stretches tight across his broad shoulders and heat seems to prickle beneath my skin now that we're alone.

Before they left, Ruby's eyes had found mine, silently questioning what I thought about Ash's proposed change of plans. My slight smile and nod were obviously a surprise to her. After all, I hadn't exactly made it a secret that I didn't want to do this and that she was forbidden from leaving me alone with him for even a minute. Asher exudes good-guy energy, though, and I'm pretty sure that even if I didn't know him and I wasn't actively fantasizing about sucking his dick, I'd still feel comfortable.

The irony that I'm now turning down a gourmet dinner —previously believed to be the only upside to this evening apart from the paycheck—in favor of sipping wine while talking to my date isn't lost on me.

It's pretty unfortunate timing that the moment they're gone, my stomach growls loudly enough to be heard over the clammer of the restaurant. Mortified, I glance at Asher to make sure he didn't catch it, but find him staring back at me, eyes glinting in amusement. "I might be hungry," I admit, my cheeks heating. The only thing I've eaten all day is coffee and a two-day-old bran muffin that tasted like cardboard.

"I am too," he confesses with a sheepish, crooked grin that makes my heart flutter. A silent understanding passes between us, a confirmation that he wanted to be alone with me and I wanted to be alone with him. He's interested, I'm interested, and now Ruby and Liam are gone. The night is ours.

Like he's thinking the same thing I am, Asher clears his throat, shifting slightly. "What, *um,* kind of food do you like?"

"Anything. I'm not picky," I say, probably too quickly. It's not terribly feminist of me to hope he pays, but I can't imagine myself being able to afford the kind of restaurants that Asher probably frequents. The hotdog stand I spotted on the corner when Ruby and I got off the subway is probably the closest to fine dining I can afford right now.

He hesitates, like he's steeling himself for whatever it is he wants to say. "I'd like to buy you dinner. Something you'll love."

Oh.

Has anyone ever said something like that to me? Ever? I don't have to think very hard to know that the answer is a definitive *hell nope,* but that doesn't explain why him saying it makes it a little hard to breathe.

I bite my lip, scrambling for an even faintly cultured answer to that question. I wasn't lying when I said I wasn't picky; I've lived on whatever's around for my entire life. Until college, I had no idea fast-food burgers or frozen lasagna weren't considered fine dining. Places with multiple forks and real tablecloths seemed like they existed only in the movies and I—

"I have no idea," I admit when I can't put off replying

any longer. "I haven't tried a whole lot. I'm not sure I even have a favorite food that isn't cereal. My family didn't have money while I was growing up, and now I'm putting myself through school—"

"You don't have to explain." Asher brushes off my embarrassment firmly. A mischievous grin pulls at the corners of his lips as he rises to his feet and, without another word, holds out a hand for me. Taking it is practically an involuntary response, and so is allowing him to help me to my feet and guide me through the lounge, never once slowing down to explain. Warmth spreads up my arm from the place our skin is touching, and I feel my breath catch when he looks back at me.

He looks so pleased with himself, grinning broadly and full of boyish enthusiasm.

"Where are we going?" I finally manage to ask, once we've gotten our coats and Asher has taken my hand again—not bothering with the pair of leather gloves the coat-check woman handed him—leading the way back through The Witt's opulent lobby and out onto the cold street.

It's January in New York, a miserable, freezing month where the entire city seems to be covered in sludge or dirty snow. I've never been more excited to be here, though. How many hours of the day do I spend just... *existing*? Even taking the time to grab a coffee with Ruby makes the naggy workaholic in the back of my head shift restlessly, and guilt sours what should be a good time. Tonight, though, there's no guilt or nagging voice to be found, and I can't stop smiling.

Asher pauses beneath The Witt's brightly lit marquee, gazing down at me, and I watch the words he was about to speak fade away. I can finally make out the color of his eyes.

They're a bright, pale blue, and I feel my pulse stutters as they dart down to my lips and back up.

The muscles in my lower belly tighten. Is he going to kiss me? Right now?

I'm not opposed to that plan. Actually, I'm pretty freakin' excited about it, and my heart flutters as his grasp on my hand tightens. We're standing so close that the vapor from our breath curls together in the freezing air, and the heady, masculine scent of his cologne makes heat pool in the lowest part of my belly.

Holy hell, he smells so good. What is it about men's cologne that makes your knees weak?

Asher is the first one to pull himself out of whatever trance we were temporarily locked in. "I'm sorry." He shakes his head slightly. "You're so beautiful, I can't stop looking at you."

Oh. Wow. Okay, then.

My answering laugh sounds wispy as I shift my hand, twining our fingers together as we set off again. It should be weird, holding hands with a near stranger, but it isn't. It feels good to let him lead, to take my brain out of my skull for a few precious moments and enjoy my life. Physically, the sensation of his bigger, rougher fingers woven through mine is strangely intimate and sensual. The warmth of his skin travels through my veins, warming me from the inside out.

Our destination turns out to be much closer than I expected. We've barely walked twenty feet past The Witt before Asher is tugging me through the door of an Italian deli. He lets go of my hand to snatch a paper menu from the counter. "Okay." He leans close to me, showing me something on the paper.

"Okay?" I echo, breathless.

"I've been here a few times. So, an amateur would pick the meatball sub, and they wouldn't be wrong. It's an excellent sandwich." Asher draws his finger across the menu to another line, and I should really be focusing on what he's telling me, but I'm too distracted by the scent of his *freakin' cologne*. Does he just spray himself down with testosterone every day and wait for the pheromones to draw in sensible, virgin college girls to turn them into sex-crazed demons?

Surely I'm not the only woman in this restaurant fighting off visions of ripping off that bow tie. How could anyone *not* be attracted to this man?

Lifting my eyes, I find him already looking at me and my stomach flip-flops at the return of that same adorable, crooked smile. "This one here has this sauce, it's—just trust me. It's fantastic."

It takes me an embarrassing amount of time to remember that we're talking about sandwiches.

I nod, just in time for the guy behind the counter to ask what we want. Asher orders, my arm pressed to his, and I can feel the heat radiating off his body, even through our winter coats. He's so much bigger than me. Is it weird to find that hot? Probably not, but it *might* be weird to wonder if he's so big *everywhere* and—Wow. I'm completely out of control.

I'm so wrapped up in him that I don't even consider where we're going to eat, until Asher collects our food in a bag and pays the guy at the counter. "Come on," He murmurs, placing a hand on the small of my back and guiding me back outside.

Again, we barely make it a few feet before I'm pulled into a taco place and into line behind a few other people. There are no menus here, just a big chalkboard listing off the place's offerings above the cash register. I look to Asher questioningly, and he chuckles. "We're going to try everything."

My eyebrows lift in surprise. "*Everything?*"

"Well, not *everything*," he amends sheepishly. "There's, unfortunately, only a finite amount of room in the human stomach. But I think we can sample at least six different cuisines to start narrowing it down."

"Narrowing what down?"

A large hand curls around my waist, and my knees seriously get weak as he leans forward to speak in my ear, his five o'clock stubble rasping over my cheek. "Your favorite food."

To my dying day, I'll never know how I keep myself from melting into a puddle on the spot.

The level of attraction I feel toward this man is borderline terrifying. "Are you always like this?" I find myself asking, unable to help myself. I'm a little afraid that I'm being swept away by the practiced routine of a career fuckboy. I already care about him way too much, and the whole lying about his job thing isn't exactly promising. This thing between us *feels* real, but what if I'm just inexperienced and naïve? What if he does this all the time? I know nothing about Doctor Roth's personal life, and now I'm plunged neck-deep into it.

Ash's head tilts to the side questioningly. We're so lost in our own little world that the guy behind us in line has to clear his throat loudly to make us realize the person in front of us has moved up. We shuffle forward, and Asher asks quietly, "Like what?"

"Sweet," I answer promptly, my voice barely above a whisper. "Funny. Charming. You must, *you know*, date a lot." I say the last bit sheepishly, because I have absolutely no business quizzing this man, who is clearly only here for a good time, about his dating habits. He isn't wearing a wedding ring, and I've never seen any evidence of a wife around his office... I have to trust that my instincts aren't completely off about him being a good guy, but still. This whole situation proves that guys can be dangerous too.

In fact, for me, good guys might be the most dangerous.

Asher draws me closer. "No. I don't date a lot," he clarifies calmly, and I suck in a shallow gasp as his thumb begins to move, tracing back and forth over the curve of my waist. "I was in a long-term relationship which ended a while back, and there's been no one since then."

Heat pools in my core, and shifting slightly, I can feel wetness spreading over my new lace panties. When I find the courage to look up and meet his gaze, those pale-blue eyes seem darker than they were only a few minutes ago. "I wasn't trying to pry."

He ignores my clumsy attempt to pass my non-question off as something other than what it was. "I'm probably too old for you to consider sweet or funny or charming." There's a low warning in his voice that does *not* help the panties situation. This is his way of testing the waters, of making it clear that this is not a platonic chat, and seeing if I'm bothered by the age difference.

Something low in my belly tightens, like there's a hook trying to tug me right into him.

Yeah, no. Not bothered.

I exhale raggedly, staring up at him from beneath my eyelashes. I'm so far out of my depth here. Aside from a sloppy, uncomfortable first kiss in the ninth grade, I've never even put my lips on a man's. Nobody wants to ask out the girl in the ratty clothes and hair that smells of lice shampoo. Guys have asked me out before, mostly in the last year or so, but I'm usually so shocked that I say no before even considering it properly.

That, and I've been quietly pining for the man currently standing beside me for years now. A man who clearly isn't looking for anything long term, as he's pretending he doesn't live a subway ride away from here.

This whole situation is a recipe for heartbreak, but my body doesn't seem to have the same qualms as the rest of me. At the very first opportunity, all those hormones I've been bottling up have come rushing to the surface. I'm a hot mess. If he asked, I'd probably strip naked and lay on top of the take-out counter.

Right about now, Ruby would be calling me a thirsty bitch, and she wouldn't be wrong.

Emboldened, I curl closer to him, pressing myself into his side. "I don't mind. Do you?"

The heat that flares in Asher's eyes makes it clear he knows exactly what I'm doing. Ahead of us, the line moves up, and as he speaks in a low hush to the woman taking our order, the hand wrapped around my waist doesn't relax for even a second.

My whole world has tilted on its axis, and I don't think I breathe properly until we're back outside. The cold air clears my head of the daze I'd been in inside the cozy, incredible-smelling restaurant, with the warmth of Asher's body bleeding into mine. Everything feels so much more real when you're cold.

Asher's stubble scrapes over the sensitive skin beside my ear as he leans down to speak quietly, an edge to his voice. "Two down." We set off again, just as snowflakes begin to fall, swirling like golden stars beneath the street lights. "Four to go."

It's probably the setting—a dark street in New York

with the scent of a storm filling my lungs and icy air biting at my cheeks—but just for a moment, my mind wanders to the night we met. Over the years, whenever I've stopped to consider the sheer improbability of our chance encounter, it's made me feel a little optimistic about the universe. Maybe that's what's happening again, and for the second time in my life I should give in and trust my instincts. Maybe—*just maybe*—meeting Asher Roth will change everything twice.

ASHER

I DIDN'T THINK this through.

I didn't think this through.

I really fucking didn't think this through.

This woman is incredible. We've barely spent a few hours together, and already I would pull out my own molars just to spend more time with her.

She's too young for me—*way* too young for me—but every time I catch a glimpse of her little smile when she looks at me, it gets harder to remember that. It's not only the physical attraction either, though that's certainly present in abundance. She's... uncommonly kind. Guarded, certainly, but some things can't be hidden. Her goodness radiates through whatever or whoever hurt her, warming every single person we come in contact with.

The woman who took our order for pad thai beamed when Adina complimented her hair.

Waiting in line for barbecue, the stressed-looking mother with two toddlers in line behind us sagged in relief when my beautiful date offered to step aside for her to go first. Then, a few minutes later, looked close to tears when

Adina knelt down and sang a song about a duck for the entertainment of her kids so she could order dinner uninterrupted.

This is one night, *it has to be*, but I'm not thinking about fucking her. Or, at least, I'm not *only* thinking about fucking her. She's gorgeous, a miraculous combination of every physical feature I find most attractive in a woman, but that's only the half of it. I find myself obsessed with the gentle curve of her smile and the way her hand fits in mine.

She's perfect.

Even in my limited experience, I know attraction like this doesn't happen every day. All evening, I've felt like I'm floating, somehow able to ditch the million pounds of self-inflicted guilt and pressure normally weighing me down. For once, I'm not thinking about the practice, or my breakup with Lindsey, or any of the other shit I find to heap guilt on myself. I'm having fun, and this is the most effortless interaction I've ever had with a member of the opposite sex.

As the hostess at the bar and grill hands us our sixth take-out bag, I find myself suddenly and brutally plummeting back to Earth.

"This is an insane amount of food." Adina laughs as we retreat onto the street, oblivious to my sudden panic. Both of us are holding a jumble of bags, each containing a dish or two from the random assortment of restaurants we passed. We stop just outside the bright neon-lit window of the bar and grill, looking at each other.

What now?

Inviting her back to my hotel room to eat seems forward, but we can't exactly sit on a bench in this weather. She doesn't even know my real fucking job. That "move" felt low when Liam did it. I should have corrected him, should have passed it off as a bad joke, but I'd been so befuddled by the angel sitting beside me that the moment slipped away. That, and, as much as I'm ashamed to admit it to myself, I liked the idea of being someone else. Someone *better*.

This version of Asher Roth is confident and funny, a man capable of catching the eye of a gorgeous younger woman. He doesn't have a mediocre career and a fear of commitment. He hasn't been celibate for so long that he's practically forgotten what it feels like to be inside a woman.

None of tonight is what I expected. It's only been a few hours, but something has shifted deep inside me, a cosmic event set in motion with final ramifications yet to be known. Nothing can come of it, of course. She's half my age, and most of what she knows about me is a lie.

I might like her, I might want her, but I can't offer more than that.

Despite all the time that's passed since we left, we're still only a block away from the hotel. "There's a table in my room." My voice is strained and unsure. Of course, I want to get her back there. Of course, I want to be alone with her, to have her all to myself, but I think I'd rather die than make her uncomfortable.

Adina doesn't *seem* uncomfortable, though. On the contrary, her lips part slightly. Pressed against me like she is, I don't miss the slight tremor running through her body. A tremor that I instinctively know has nothing to do with the cold as slowly, shyly, she nods.

The knowledge I've had that effect on her is intoxicating; it emboldens me.

Holy fuck. Okay. Yes.

She keeps close to me, our arms brushing as we walk, until we get back to the familiar brightly lit marquee outside The Witt. The doorman's eyes fall to the obscene assortment of take-out bags we're holding, eyebrows rising in interest. Adina, not missing it, plucks one at random off her hand with a musical laugh and offers it to him. "We have so much. Would you mind?"

He doesn't mind.

My heart thunders against my rib cage as I lead the way to the row of gleaming brass elevator doors along the back of the lobby, shifting the bags to one hand so I can rest the other against the small of her back.

"This place is amazing," Adina whispers, then blushes, as if it's embarrassing that she's never been to a five-star hotel. I have no idea what her background is, and I'm not sure I want to. Learning more about this woman feels dangerous.

Tongue-tied, I guide her into the first elevator that opens, half worried we'll run into Liam and Ruby and this spell will be broken. Touching her is like a drug; ever since I got that first hit, I can't seem to help myself from indulging whenever possible. "Rumor has it, it's haunted. If you believe in that kind of thing." I hit the button for my floor, and the doors slide shut.

The moment they do, it's like all the air has been sucked from the tiny room. We're alone—*really alone*—for the first time.

This must be dawning on Adina as well, because over the quiet classical music playing above our heads, I hear her exhale shakily. Her eyes are fixed resolutely on the back of the doors, and I follow her gaze, meeting those star-tlingly green eyes in the mirrored surface. All night we've been shying away from looking at each other directly for too long, making do with hurried glances and pretending not to notice when the other is staring.

I'm nearly two decades older than this woman. I have graying hair and lines at the corners of my eyes. In honor of Liam's hatred of it, I wore a fucking *bow tie* tonight. What was I thinking? Meanwhile, Adina looks like a goddess, practically glowing with beauty and youth. I'm old enough to be her father. We *should* look ridiculous together.

Those insecurities fade away with what I see in the mirrored doors, though. The couple reflected there... *fits.*

Holy shit.

The tiny room spins around me, but still I can't look away from those wide, green eyes. Connection is crackling to life between us. Unable to hold myself back anymore, I turn, backing her into the nearest wall.

Adina's soft gasp of surprise goes right to my cock as I press myself against her, sealing our bodies together.

Bags crinkle, our breathing is ragged, and somewhere in the back of my mind I can still hear the quiet, bland classical music playing above us. None of it matters.

Adina's sharp little chin lifts, her lips parting in silent offering.

An offering that I'd have to be the world's biggest fool not to accept.

Groaning quietly, I bow forward, brushing my lips over hers. The ghost of a kiss. It's chaste and almost shy, a bizarre juxtaposition to the fact that my painfully hard cock is pressed shamelessly against her stomach. Christ, I want her so badly. I can't remember ever—I stop the thought in its tracks, guilt infringing on the cloud of blind lust I've been floating on.

Adina's free hand creeps up to curl around the back of my neck, and she pulls me back down to meet her lips again.

This kiss is deeper than the last, but just as slow. We're

both clumsy and unsure, but it doesn't take us long to find our rhythm, melting into each other so naturally it's like we've been doing this for years instead of minutes. This whole night, from the first moment I saw her in the lounge to every moment after... All of it was building toward this. If I was obsessed before, it's nothing compared to the possessive animal clawing its way to the surface now.

For the first time since Lindsey and I broke up, and probably long before that, I'm allowing myself to be selfish.

Then again, *allowing* makes it seem like a choice. Every second we spend entwined against the elevator wall makes it clearer that there's nothing optional about this. I've never needed anyone the way I need her right now, and I refuse to allow my own guilt to ruin any part of this. Adina whimpers, arching her body into mine.

I take the hint.

Sliding a leg between her thighs, she melts against me with a throaty whine, grinding her hot little cunt over me. There's material between us, but I can tell how wet she is. Almost in unison, the take-out bags fall to the floor at our sides. Our hands are free now, and I don't know what feels better: her touching me or me touching her.

I'm only dimly aware of the ground moving beneath us; it seems like such an unimportant detail. Or it does until the lift chimes, signaling our arrival at another floor.

Fucking damn it.

By the time an elderly man steps onto the elevator, Adina and I are hurriedly gathering up the dropped bags, her face flaming. It couldn't be more obvious what we were doing in here, especially when I have to reach past him to press the button for my floor again. With every passing second, the greedy, possessive feeling inside me coils tighter. When our silent companion finally steps off, the doors have barely closed again before I all but launch myself at Adina.

She's right there with me, moaning into my mouth as I press her against the wall, kissing frantically. The taste of her—fuck. She's so sweet. It would be so easy to get lost in her, to stand here, our bodies pressed tight, for hours. I must have some presence of sound mind remaining, though, because when the elevator doors open at my floor this time, I wrench myself back and slap my free hand out to prevent them from closing again.

Adina gazes at me, her pupils wide. Panting, she fumbles with her bags and follows as I back out of the elevator, not taking our eyes off one another for even a second.

The room Liam gave me for the night is halfway down the hall, an opulent suite which must ordinarily cost a fortune. It's befitting the successful businessman Liam told her I am, but the moment we go through the door, Adina seems to falter. She draws herself back against the wall, watching silently as I shut the door and hurry to flick on the lights in the living area. All the passion that was burning so fiercely between us only a few seconds ago has gone cold.

"Saw a cockroach over there, watch out," I attempt to joke, but the only response I get is the corner of her lips lifting into a tight smile as she scans the room. "Come on." It's an effort to begin moving again, and I feel unnatural and self-conscious as I lead the way over to the small dining area. The suite is so quiet that even the sound of the bags being set down on the table seems unnaturally loud.

Edging closer, Adina bites her lip, eyes still roaming over the room we're in. I can see it happening—she's shrinking into herself, trying to disappear just like she was when I first saw her in the lounge downstairs, and I won't have it.

"Adina." Looking up at the sound of her name, she grimaces apologetically.

"Sorry." Her hands fumble with the buttons of her coat and the strap of her purse as she sets them to the side and slides into the chair across from mine. She keeps her eyes down as she busies herself with opening the dishes we collected. As someone who never quite managed to be self-sufficient enough to actually cook himself dinner, I'm well-versed in the range of cuisines in New York. We've assembled an impressive cross section in such a limited geographical area, but something inside me pinches at the thought of all the other things I'd like to have her try.

One night, I remind myself, almost viciously, as Adina reaches tentatively for a street taco. This is supposed to be a fucking rebound. She dates rich men for money; she wouldn't be interested in me if she knew I wear a sparkly lab coat and give away more procedures than I bill.

"Wait." I shake myself, then reach into the paper bag it came from to pull out a sauce packet.

Squeezing hot sauce onto someone's taco *could* be a fun euphemism, or it could be the least sexy chivalrous act of all time. At the very least, in this case, it has the benefit of breaking through Adina's nervousness. She lets out a reluctant giggle as the sauce comes out unevenly in one place and drips onto her thumb.

The sight of her pink tongue darting out to lick it away hits me like a physical blow.

Mouth dry, I sit back, watching as she takes a bite and groans softly, her eyes dropping closed in pleasure.

Christ, how am I going to get through this without mauling her? Every last thing this woman does seems to make my cock harder, and my imagination comes up with a million ways to make her feel good. It's been so fucking long, and I've certainly never felt this gnawing, bone-deep need before.

"I don't know how any of this will top that." Adina sighs happily, successfully lightening the sudden tension in the room. She sets the taco down after her third bite, scanning the other boxes appraisingly.

My own face splits in a smile as I watch. She was hesitant about this before, maybe put off by the decadence of the whole thing, but now I can feel her enthusiasm building.

I can't remember the last thing I've enjoyed as much as spoiling this woman.

Like she can feel my eyes on her, Adina looks up, and my cock twitches as she catches her lip between her teeth. "Aren't—I mean. Aren't you going to eat anything?"

Instantly, her tight, too-young-for-me cunt comes to mind.

I nod. "Yes." Reaching over to her side of the table, I take the half finished taco and bite into the side her lips just touched without hesitation. It *is* good, but not as good as what I want from her.

The quiet room presses in around us. Fireworks could go off right outside the window and I doubt I would notice a thing. Neither of us speak, quietly eating our way through a bit of everything until, finally, Adina closes the last take-out box and leans back in her chair, gazing at me.

"You're looking at me a lot." Her quiet, teasing comment makes me chuckle. What the hell does she expect?

My chair scrapes over the wood floors as I push away

from the table. Fuck it. She's attracted to me and I'm obsessed with her, so I'm going for it. "Come here."

For a moment, I think she won't. We stare at each other, tension crackling in the air between us. Finally, she stands and moves around the table, not stopping until she's in front of me. "Asher…"

I don't give her time to feel self-conscious. My hands come out, boldly pulling her into my lap. Adina gasps quietly in surprise, hands landing on my shoulders. Her body is warm and soft in my arms, and she smells so good —clean and sweet. I love the way she fits against me, small and firm and exquisitely feminine. My arms tighten, gathering her closer, and every little rustle of clothing or ragged exhale that I hear is another can of gasoline thrown on the fire burning me from the inside out.

Adina doesn't hesitate, tilting her head back to kiss me like it's a foregone conclusion, like this was always—*always* —going to happen.

She wants me.

This is slower than our last kiss, but hotter too. Within seconds, her lips have fallen open, her moan muffled by my tongue. There's something heady and intense behind the tentative exploration, about how much effort it's costing both of us to hold back.

Adina's quiet, needy whimper snaps whatever's left of my self-control.

Growling, I arch my body over hers, tilting her back so far she's forced to cling to me to avoid falling. My hands find her perfect, round ass, and the noise I make is something akin to a snarl. Is there a single inch of this woman that isn't tailor made to turn me on? She feels incredible, barely able to do more than hold on as I devour her mouth and grope her tight, college-girl ass.

I bet if I pushed my hand between those beautiful thighs, I'd find her slick, swollen and dripping for my attention.

When I move to do it, though, Adina stiffens.

It's like someone has thrown a bucket of ice water over me. "Is something wrong?" I pant, drawing back so I can see her face.

She's still panting. "It's kind of embarrassing." Her expression tightens. "It's just... I've never done this before."

"Done this" meaning have sex with a man she was paid to date? Or—*fuck*.

My cock, which is hard as a rock and pressed against the bottom of her thigh, twitches. Something is rising inside me, a savage sort of arousal and possessiveness, the urge to *claim*. I'm too fucking old to be turned on by her inexperience, or to imagine how it would look to see my thickness sliding into her.

My—admittedly battered—conscience puts a stop to the fantasies quickly. Or tries to.

Before I can even think of how to respond to this, Adina continues, her eyes widening in embarrassment and alarm. "I know you're not looking for anything serious! I just—oh god. I don't know why I told you that." Her cheeks are practically glowing, they're so pink. If I weren't so torn up inside, I'd be even more taken with her.

She's so fucking cute.

I clear my throat. "I'm sorry. I shouldn't have—" I look down at our current position, bodies entwined atop the chair, my erection still pressing into her ass.

Adina's eyes go wide. "I sat on your lap! I kind of knew what I was getting into and I was fully on board for all of it. I liked it. I guess I just need..." She trails off, looking mortified.

"What do you need?" I lower my head to kiss her shoulder, still reeling with this information that is somehow painful and intoxicating at once. She's a virgin. How could I possibly ask her to give that up for a single night in a hotel room with a man she doesn't love?

A man who's been lying to her all night.

Despite the wild, possessive instincts Adina has so unexpectedly brought out in me, I also know I wouldn't be able to live with myself if I took more than this. It's so difficult to pull away from her. Just as touching her came as easy as breathing, my entire body tightens in protest of my putting distance between us.

"I'm sorry." I barely recognize my own voice, it's so rough. "You deserve so much more than one night."

Adina is frozen in my lap, but at my words, she gets unsteadily to her feet.

"I should go," she whispers, keeping her eyes on the floor as she moves around the table to grab her coat and bag. "Thank you for everything. It's been so nice getting to know you." Every word is painfully formal, and the warm familiarity, which so recently existed between us, is gone. Despite her measured tone, though, she has to try at least three times to get her arm through the sleeve of her coat.

She's just as rattled by this as I am.

I stand too, gazing at her profile as cold dread seeps through me. Does she think I don't want her?

"Do you want…" I cough, scrambling to read the situation correctly. "Would you *like* to stay?"

Adina shakes her head immediately, fumbling with her coat. "No! I mean, this was fun. Oh gosh, I'm being super weird." Pausing, she lets out a long breath before finally turning to face me. "I'm sorry. You're totally right. Most people don't have a one-night stand for their first time. It's *a lot,* I totally get it. I should wait for someone who wants... all that."

My stomach churns because I do want *all that,* and the thought of some faceless stranger putting his hands on Adina is abhorrent to me. I have no right to be this affected, but I am.

I need to let her go, but I don't want to leave it like this.

She's turning to the door when I appear behind her, catching her elbow in my hand. "Adina." I search the adorable, surprised look on her face, and it feels like something in my chest is tugging me right in her direction. I swallow, trying to ignore it. "For the record, I do want you to stay. More than anything. I just... I wouldn't want you to regret this."

Me. I don't want her to regret *me.*

Adina's lips curve into a gentle, sad smile. It tugs at my fucking heart. Drawing forward, she places her hand on my chest, directly over my heart. Its rhythm stalls when she kisses my cheek, lingering just long enough for me to breathe in the scent of her hair for the first time.

She smells like honey and wildflowers.

THERE'S a blister on my heel, my heart is aching worse than the ankle I rolled trying to avoid vomit on the sidewalk, and the fairy tale is well and truly over.

Cinderella had her fun at the ball, and now it's time to turn back into a homeless college student with two jobs.

I bet this is exactly how she would have felt, though— hollowed out and disappointed, wondering if her whole magical night was some kind of fever dream. Going back to scrubbing toilets and dreaming about what your life will be like is a lot harder once you've gotten a glimpse behind the curtain.

Not that I expect my life to be anything like tonight once I graduate. Nobody becomes a social worker thinking they'll be able to afford staying in places like The Witt or ordering dishes from six different restaurants just for the fun of trying them. Besides, I'm not feeling this way because I have to say goodbye to the expensive dress, heels, fancy food, and glamorous hotel.

I didn't want to say goodbye to Asher, and I haven't quite worked out why I didn't stay.

It wasn't that I didn't want to. I *really* wanted to. Every single hormone-ridden cell in my body was screaming at me to pull my dress up, bend over the table, and let Asher Roth do whatever he wanted to me. In the elevator, when I felt his erection pressing against my stomach, it was like I fell under a spell. I needed him. As though rubbing myself all over the man was as essential as keeping my heart beating.

Realizing I made him hard was hands down the hottest moment of my life, which was quickly eclipsed by a new hottest moment of my life when he let me grind myself all over it. I've never felt like that, *ever*, and the lingering dampness of my panties is a cruel reminder of how good it felt to have his hands on me.

Even now, hours later, I still feel so... unsettled.

My virginity isn't something I'm attached to, but I always imagined having sex as one of those abstract, far-off things. I was getting around to the whole thing, but it wasn't a rush. I'm not completely innocent; I've read my fair share of spicy books and watched porn a few times. I've fallen asleep on the couch in Asher's office and dreamed that my tall, handsome boss came in and woke me up with his head between my legs... Yet when I had my chance to have that for real, I went running for the hills.

I pause at the top of the stairs leading down into the subway station, my hand curling tightly over the metal railing.

After the childhood I had, being cautious is practically an involuntary response now. The only times I've ever been brave were when I absolutely had to. Keeping my head down, working hard, and staying on the right path is safe. Going back to Doctor Roth's office and not having sex with him is safe. He didn't want anything serious, that much was obvious, and my heart isn't exactly *uninvested*.

Feet heavy, I start the descent into the subway station. Each step down the grungy stairwell seems to get a little harder.

Would it be so wrong for me to just... go for it?

He wanted me, at least for tonight. Doctor Asher Roth will never fall in love with me, not when he finds out the truth—or *some* of the truth—of where I came from. The man quite literally saw me cuddled up in the trash with no hair and a bloody face. He pays me to scrub the toilets in his practice and writes notes making sure I can afford my books for school. Allison is a victim in his eyes, and after tonight, Adina is a play thing.

I'm running on autopilot as I reach the platform. A few dozen people are waiting, bundled up in winter gear. No one looks my way as I lean against the grimy tile wall, flashes of tonight playing in my mind.

Seeing Asher across The Witt's lounge for the first time, and feeling something warm and dangerous rising inside me.

Curling into his side as we waited for Italian food, so wrapped up in each other we didn't notice that the hostess had called his name three times.

The heat of his body as he pressed mine into the wall of the elevator.

Sucking in an unsteady breath, I stare blankly at the station wall across from me. Fresh wetness is spreading over my panties as yet another slideshow of what-ifs plays in my mind's eye. I left because I was afraid, because I thought I would regret sleeping with him. How could it have not occurred to me that I might regret *not* sleeping with him?

Am I going to be like this forever? Hiding away from

what I really want because I'm afraid it will bite me in the ass? Holding myself apart from people because I'm too scared to get close?

The thought makes something defiant rise inside me. *No.* No, I don't want that. I don't want to sacrifice any more of my life to the people who hurt me. Three years ago, I did the ultimate hard, brave thing... I ran. I ran and I never went back. Even when it seemed impossible, even when I thought dying would be better than living and that I would never matter to anyone, *I didn't go back.*

This might have been my only chance to be with a man I have feelings for. I haven't even been gone for thirty minutes and I already regret not being brave. Tonight doesn't have to be over, though. It's not too late. If I can step away from the safety and familiarity of what I should be doing right now, maybe I'll have one less regret.

Maybe the prince won't notice Cinderella is a maid if she takes all her clothes off?

My train pulls in and I stand stock still, watching passengers get off. Others get on, and I don't move, excitement humming in my veins.

As the doors close, I've already turned back toward the entrance of the station, following the small crowd of people making their way up onto the street.

Hell. Yes. I'm doing this. I'm seriously doing this. *Holy crap.*

The walk back to The Witt seems to take a lot less time than the walk to the subway station. I don't notice the pain in my ankle or the blister on my heel, too busy trying to work out if I'm excited or terrified.

It never occurred to me that my first time would be anything like this. Did I imagine myself spread out over

Doctor Roth's desk while he fucks me in his sparkly lab coat? Yes. Many times. I clearly have issues.

I definitely didn't picture myself marching down one of the most expensive streets in New York, wearing a dress that probably costs more than what I make in a week—I didn't dare look at the price tag when Ruby made me try it on—preparing to knock on that same dentist's hotel room door. Asher doesn't have feelings for me. He isn't looking for a relationship with the broke college girl who was desperate enough to get paid for a date, and he certainly won't be falling for the girl who vacuums his office.

This is *one night*, and I want him enough that it's worth it.

The doorman standing outside the hotel is thankfully the one who I gave food to only an hour ago. He holds open the door for me, standing back with a cheerful nod in my direction.

I nod back, trying not to make eye contact with anyone as I rush across the lobby to the line of brassy elevators. I can't shake the worry that I'm doing something wrong by being here, as if I'm trespassing somehow. Places like this are as foreign to me as the moon. It's almost *more* bizarre that no one stops me. Can't they look at me and tell that I don't belong?

Apparently not.

The doors to the elevator close behind me just as a hotel employee approaches, and my heart stalls. All he does is smile respectfully, though, stepping back to allow me the lift to myself. The moment the doors close, I collapse against the back wall. Everything seems to be moving at warp speed, and the ride up to the eighth floor takes only seconds. Then I'm in the hall and standing in front of Ash's door, the final barrier keeping me safe from the unknown.

I could leave right now. He would never know, but —*damn it*—I would! I would know that I was a big fat chicken who walked away from what she wanted, not once, but twice.

Not giving myself time to back down, I raise my fist and knock.

Every inch of my skin is suddenly humming, sparked to life as the adrenaline flowing through my bloodstream. This wild, restless feel*ing isn't me*. I've never experienced anything even close to this intense, but when I hear the lock sliding out of place and the door pulls open, all concerns about what *is* or *isn't* me evaporate.

Holy hell.

He just got out of the shower. His hair is damp and tousled, his skin is flushed, and he's wearing nothing but a towel slung low on his hips. My eyes have a mind of their own, raking over his broad, defined chest and flat, hard stomach. They follow the trail of dark-brown hair from below his belly button to where it vanishes beneath the towel.

My pulse skyrockets. The feeling of a hook catching low in my belly and dragging me toward Asher is so intense that my hand presses over it.

"Adina." The way he says my name... *God.*

Mouth dry, I look back up to meet his eyes, and they seem so much darker than I remember. The heat from the shower seems to be radiating off his skin, warming me even standing two feet away. I can smell the fresh, clean scent of soap on his skin and see tiny droplets on his shoulders that must have fallen from his hair.

I swallow, pressing my hand more firmly against the tugging below my belly button. If I thought things were intense between us earlier, there's no comparison to how I feel now. It's like we're locked in orbit, drawn together by even the air between us.

I'm wound so tight, I think I'll shatter if he doesn't touch me soon.

"Adina," Asher repeats, urgent now, and he seems just as incapable of looking away from me as I am from him. It's all I can do to stop myself from whimpering when he leans forward, bracing a defined forearm on the doorway. "What are you doing here?" He doesn't look unhappy to see me, though, and this gives me the shot of confidence I need to tell him exactly why I came back.

"I was wondering… wondering if you'd have sex with me." Wow. I can't believe those words just came out of my mouth. Ash's jaw goes slack with shock, like he can't quite believe it either. I don't have time to be embarrassed, though. Down the hall, the elevator chimes and, glancing in that direction, his hand finds mine. He tugs me inside, closing the door behind us.

Admittedly, I haven't been in a ton of fancy hotel rooms, but this one still seems faintly ridiculous in how nice it is. The shock doesn't hit me like it did last time, though, because I have bigger and better things on my mind. Mainly, the sight of his nearly naked body silhouetted by the New York skyline in the windows behind him.

Summoning all the brand-new bravery I mustered up to come back here, I step forward and spread my hand over his warm, bare chest. His heart pulses unevenly beneath my hand "*Adina.*" Asher growls warningly, his pulse thudding erratically beneath my palm. "I can't promise you anything after tonight. I have—*oh fuck.* What do you want from me, angel?"

Angel.

Why do I like that so much?

Blowing out a long breath, I draw closer, greedily inhaling the scent of his clean skin. "I don't care." My voice has lost some of its bravado. I've never done this before, never done *anything* before, and the truth is I have only the vaguest ideas of what I want Asher to do to me. All I know is I want him—*need him*, even—and I'm prepared to beg. "Please?"

We're so close I can feel the heat radiating from his body. He's *hot*, scorching me through the thick material of my coat and dress. When I close the last few inches between us to press myself against him, I'm so dizzy with lust I might faint. Like in the elevator earlier, my breasts brush his chest, and his hardness drags against my stomach.

Except now, we're alone. We have hours and hours ahead of us, and we can do anything we want with it.

Asher makes a rough, desperate sound. "You left, Adina."

"I came back," I argue, barely keeping myself from moaning as a muscular thigh slides between mine, pressing directly against my throbbing sex. It's the same position we were in earlier in the elevator, but this is so much better. The urge to rock against him is too much, and I can't help squirming just a little. "I regretted it, and I came back. I want this—*you*—even if it's just this once."

Without warning, he gathers me closer and I moan, my clit pulsing against the new pressure.

I'm about to lean forward and kiss the hollow of his throat when a big hand nudges my chin up and forces me to meet his eyes. It's nearly the exact same position we were in before I left. We're getting a redo, and—

"I can't give you more than this, sweet girl," he warns me, his voice a low growl. "I won't take you on dates or buy you pretty things like Liam does for your friend. We might never see each other again after tonight. *Are. You. Sure?*"

Something pinches painfully inside me at his words and warning bells are ringing, but I still don't falter in my decision. "*Yes.*"

Asher's hands find my waist, holding me so hard it's almost painful, and the whimper I've been holding back since he opened the door finally escapes my lips. We're so absorbed in each other, the fire alarm could be blaring above our heads and I doubt either of us would notice. I can't focus on anything other than the places my skin is touching his.

I expect desperate, dumb lust, for him to consume me in seconds, but that's not what Asher does. Like he's giving me every chance to walk away, my stranger kisses me so intensely that all the air in my lungs seems to vanish. My lips part instinctively, offering myself to him, and he doesn't hesitate.

His teeth drag over my bottom lip and I arch closer to him as his hands find the opening of my coat and push it off my shoulders. The sound of the fabric hitting the floor seems unnaturally loud in the still room.

Time is moving so much faster than usual. Just a few hours ago I was sitting in the library, my stomach churning with nerves about tonight, and now I feel like a brand-new person. A person who doesn't hesitate to drop her hands on Asher's bare stomach, low enough to make him groan, and run them up his chest to settle on his broad shoulders. A person who whispers raggedly in his ear when he bows forward to bite and suck my neck, "Show me how to make you feel good."

My words trigger something inside him. Grunting, Asher wrenches himself away from me and steps back toward the little living room area, crooking his finger with a sly smirk. I follow immediately, nearly stumbling over my own feet in my too high heels.

"Stop," he orders gruffly, sinking into a leather armchair. We're ten feet apart, an unbearable distance after feeling his body pressed against mine. "Take your clothes off for me, Adina. Show me what I've been picturing all night."

My stomach swoops, but my hands still tremble as I reach beneath my arm, finding the tiny pull of the hidden zipper sewn into the side of the dress. I've never felt so sexy, so desired, as I do right now. Asher leans forward, his heated gaze roaming over my body as I let the dress fall, hands biting into the arms of the chair like he's trying to restrain himself.

I wouldn't mind if he didn't.

The plunging neckline had left no room for a bra, so beneath the dress I'm wearing only a tiny black thong, that's now so wet it sticks to my skin, and flesh-colored sticky cups cradling my breasts. I go to pull them away, but Asher shakes his head. "Leave them."

I move on. Hooking my thumbs beneath the band of my panties, I drag them slowly over my thighs and allow them to fall too. As I step out of my heels onto the cold floor, there's no mistaking the raw hunger in Asher's expression. The only light in the room is coming through the windows from the street outside, but I still doubt he'll miss how ridiculously, shamelessly wet I am. Even the inside of my thighs are sticky from our make-out session by the door and the thrill of baring myself for him. A quiet gasp escapes my lips as Asher's hand finds the edge of his towel, and pulls it aside.

Oh shit.

Whoever came up with the saying "biting off more than you can chew" probably had this exact situation in mind. Asher's cock is *big*. Long and intimidatingly thick, the silky skin of his shaft gives way to the deep-purple head that's shiny from the white pre-cum beading at his slit. My thighs press together instinctively, core clenching with either need or fear. Probably a little of both.

Asher smirks, like he knows exactly what I'm thinking. "You're a smart girl, Adina. I'm sure you'll do just fine." His tone is teasing, but there's a dark fire burning in his eyes that makes me pretty confident I'm in for it. "Come here." He pats his thigh and, like he's taken control of my mind as well as my body, I obey.

I stop just in front of him, and Ash's hands reach out to trace reverently over my hips to settle on my waist. I tremble. "About sixty seconds before you knocked on that door, I was fisting my cock and coming all over the shower wall to thoughts of you."

It's a miracle I don't collapse. The thought of Asher like that—stroking himself—his beautiful face contorted in pleasure... I whimper.

He traces his thumbs over the bones of my pelvis and nods slightly, distracted. "I imagined how good it would feel to push inside you, the faces you'd make, the sounds."

Looking between us, the muscles of my core contract.

"I'm pretty sure *that's* not fitting inside me." I giggle breathlessly. Is it rude to stare at a guy's junk in a sexual situation? Because I kind of want to stare. What about pictures? I'm positive my memory isn't good enough to do this justice.

"That?" Asher teases, raising his eyebrows. Placing his hands on the backs of my knees, he guides me forward until I'm straddling him, my ass settled on his legs and the parted lips of my pussy just inches away from his shaft. "I'm sure you can do better than that."

I'm trying to focus, but his legs are spread enough that there's nothing for me to grind on or press against to relieve the almost unbearable throbbing of my clit except the massive *thing* that somehow looks even larger in proportion to my body. I swallow. "Your, your penis." The word sounds ridiculous in this context, clinical and immature.

Asher clearly agrees, because he chuckles, running his hands over my bare thighs to give my ass a playful squeeze. "Try again."

Unable to resist, I tilt forward and press my slit right over his length. Moaning in relief, I rock against him, my eyes fluttering shut. "You cock." I sigh, and Asher grunts his approval, guiding my pace over his *cock* that is now slick with my arousal. He's so much harder than I expected him to be, and I can feel every vein standing out on his shaft.

"Good girl. Fuck, you're incredible. Look at you go." He can't seem to stop touching me, running his hands over every inch of skin he can until he reaches the sticky cups covering half my breasts. It *shouldn't* be sexy, but the hungry, possessive expression on his face makes the heat building low in my core burn even hotter. I gasp as he pulls the silicone away from my skin, and he hisses his approval.

Tilting my body back, he latches onto one of my nipples, drawing it into his mouth as his hand finds the other, teasing and pulling roughly. "Oh." My lips part in a noise somewhere between a moan and a cry. I roll my hips frantically, so wet now that I slide easily over his shaft, and Ash's free hand digs into my hip to slow my movements.

"That's it." He grunts when he pulls off my nipple with a wet noise, his voice lower and rougher than ever before. I'm shaking now, my breaths coming in ragged pants as my orgasm spirals closer. "Take what you need, angel. Listen to your body. *That's it.* I've got you."

My eyes squeeze shut as my head drops back, the ends of my hair tickling my lower back. I grind harder, and for the first time, I realize how empty I feel. With a dizzying, lust-drunk burst of clarity, it occurs to me that the imposing length of Ash's cock isn't so scary anymore. It's… exciting. "Fuck me," I plead, my legs shaking with the force of the orgasm I'm barreling toward. My thighs are burning, but I'm so close. "Please, Ash. *Please!*"

A big hand comes down on my ass, slapping me so hard that I squeal, and his voice sounds like a low growl in my ear. "Be a good girl and come for daddy, then we'll discuss it."

DADDY?

Fucking *daddy*?

Where the hell did that come from? It's slightly fucked up, considering I really am old enough to be Adina's father, but any self-consciousness or regret goes out the window almost instantly. The words have barely left my mouth when Adina comes with a wail that will probably echo out into the hall, her body shaking against mine as she comes violently.

I've never seen a woman's orgasm more beautiful.

"Daddy," she whines, and I'm only vaguely aware of uttering a ragged groan in response. Lunging forward, I claim her lips with mine, devouring her as the wetness from her pussy leaks freely over my balls. Kissing Adina doesn't make me feel the way it did with any other woman. We've barely begun, and already I'm addicted.

The taste of her invades my senses, creating a pleasant, hazy buzz that vibrates through me. Her naked body is still pressed intimately against mine, but I can tell by the way she's tilting her hips up to avoid pressing her clit against me that the poor thing must be overly sensitive from the orgasm she just gave herself.

Too fucking bad.

Needing to do a hell of a lot more than this chair allows, I grasp her hips and guide her off me. I intended to stand too, to guide her toward the bed or whichever flat surface seems appealing in the moment. Now, though… Now all I can do is stare. I'm struck dumb, awed. As a fresh wave of lust slams over me, threatening to pull me under, I'm positive I'll remember the way she looks right now for the rest of my life: gazing down at me, her lips swollen and rosy nipples pebbled in the cool air of the hotel room, dark hair in disarray around her shoulders.

Tilting forward, my hands find the sides of her pale thighs. Neither of us speak as I reach back to grip her perfect, round ass and lean forward to drag my tongue over the hollow between her breasts. My fingers are dangerously close to her second hole, and I have to hold myself back from stroking her there too.

I've never felt like this. She's managed to tap into a side of me that's deeper and darker than I knew existed. For fuck's sake, she's a virgin, and I want to finger her ass? The good, respectable Doctor Roth is gone, and in his place is a dominant, possessive creature who wants to tie the beautiful virgin to his bed and fuck his cum into her all night. My orgasm in the shower was violent, more powerful than I can remember experiencing before, but already my balls are so full they ache.

This isn't want. It's pure, unadulterated need.

Adina moans throatily above me, her hands darting to my shoulders for balance as I move one hand between her legs, cupping her slick cunt.

I won't fuck her. *I won't.* We're temporary. Even if she

understands that, I can't stomach taking that from her while she believes I'm something I'm not.

I'll make her feel good. I'll make her come until she can't stand, and I will ignore the erection that is now so hard it's bordering on painful.

The sound of our ragged breathing sounds unnaturally loud in the quiet room. "How's that?" I ask, dragging my fingers over her swollen clit to her slick entrance. Slowly, without breaking eye contact, I ease a single finger past her entrance, pressing into her tight heat.

Her sexy, shocked face makes my cock throb. "Oh."

One word, one fucking syllable, and I'm prepared to abandon whatever scraps of morality I have left to watch myself fuck this woman. I'm a large man, and just the thought of my too big, too-old-for-her cock stretching her over my length is enough to torch my last rational brain cell.

My thumb finds her swollen clit and I caress it teasingly —up and down, up and down—her body responding to my touch instantly.

"Oh my god!" Adina's head falls back, hips jolting into my hand. I add a second finger, fucking her shallowly, *carefully*. The way she feels... I'd probably embarrass myself if I tried to get inside her right now; add that to the towering number of reasons we won't be having sex tonight.

God help me—I will not fucking fuck her.

I don't think I've blinked. My eyes are too busy raking over her beautiful body, hungrily memorizing the touches that make her whine or shake and the anxious way she shifts her hips against my hand. It couldn't be clearer she's inexperienced. The tightness of her cunt aside, my horny little angel needed a few minutes to adjust to my thick fingers inside her. When she does, though, the cry of ecstasy makes pre-cum drip over the head of my cock.

"Close?" I lean forward, my eyes glued to the juncture of her thighs. The sloppy, wet sounds coming from my fingers fucking her are profane, and they're getting louder by the second. I can feel her getting more excited, feel the effect I'm having on her, and my body responds in kind.

Her hands bite into my shoulders, knees almost buckling when I curve my fingers to find that spot I'm betting she didn't know existed until now. "Daddy, I'm coming, I'm—"

In the heat of the moment, I somehow forgot I'd opened that particular kinky can of worms. Hearing her say it again as she falls apart on my hand is a shock to the system. "You're so fucking beautiful." I groan, lust searing through me as I lurch to my feet, swallowing the last of her moans with a hungry kiss that makes my cock leap against her stomach.

She's soft and warm in my arms, her body pliant after two orgasms. Still, my greedy girl's arms twine around my neck the moment I begin guiding her back toward the bedroom. We never break our kiss, but with each step, my impatience mounts. A glimpse of the chaise arranged before the windows sends a dark, gleeful thrill through me.

The room is dimly lit, but it's enough that if someone in the offices across the street were to look this way, they might see the silhouette of our bodies.

I change course.

Adina squeals when I push her back onto the plush seat, tits bouncing as she sprawls out below me. I keep my eyes on her face as I lower my body over hers, feeling her thighs fall open to make room for me. "Please," she pleads, her voice barely audible over our ragged breathing and the pulsing of my own heart.

Her hands, which had found my shoulders only seconds ago, drift lower.

"Angel," I protest weakly, my body heating under her tentative touch. My cock is leaking freely between us, drawing sticky lines of pre-cum over her gently curved belly. I'm hanging on by a thread, struggling to remember all the reasons I said I wouldn't do this.

She's a virgin, and I'm a fucking liar.

She dates rich men for money, and I'm poor.

She's beautiful, kind, and hardworking; the kind of woman any man could fall in love with, and I've proven myself to be incapable of true commitment.

That last reason is admittedly looking a little flimsy in light of this new evidence. In six years with my ex, I never felt anything like the hunger and attraction Adina has sparked in me after only a few hours. I want this to be more than one night. I want to keep her. Marriage? No problem, where's the nearest church? Marriage is tame in comparison to what I would do to bind myself to this woman in every way.

This desire could swallow me whole if I let it. She's spread out beneath me, begging for it, her beautiful pussy so wet and willing. It would be the work of seconds to guide my length to her entrance and press forward. I'm so conflicted that I don't realize what she's planning until it's too late.

A small hand wraps around the base of my cock, and it's all I can do to hold myself up. *Fuck.*

Adina's breath ghosts over my lips, gazing up at me through hooded eyes. Her hand tightens, giving an experimental stroke that tears a guttural groan from deep in my chest. She pauses, a flash of worry crossing her beautiful features. "Is this okay?"

Okay?

I let out a short, choked laugh. My head drops weakly onto her shoulder and, working independently of my brain, my hips roll into her tentative grasp. "Harder," I hear myself order, and Adina obliges immediately. She works me slowly, her other hand weaving through my hair. It would be so easy to get lost in her, to allow myself to succumb to the mind-melting pleasure that is this woman's touch. She's becoming more confident, her strokes coming in time to her own breathy moans, like this is giving her every bit as much satisfaction as it is me.

My balls are already tightening, threatening to spill all over her, but I sit back on my heels at the last moment. Head spinning and cock throbbing painfully, I meet her worried gaze. Not giving her time to second-guess herself, I step back off the ottoman and drop to my knees.

She looks like a goddamn treat, thighs loose and open, offering me every inch of her precious body.

She makes me want to be selfish, *to take.*

"Oh, angel. Look at you." I wrap my hands around her thighs and drag her to the edge, bringing myself face-to-face with her pussy for the first time.

"Asher!" Adina squeaks above me, and a pair of slim hands shoot down to cover herself. "You don't have to do that."

I blink up at her, my chest heaving as I struggle to think through the haze of lust clouding my mind. Has she ever been this vulnerable with a man before? I doubt it, but even so... If I ever hear her suggest that eating this pussy is some kind of chore again, I'll put her over my knee.

Wordlessly, I take her wrists in my hands and pull them

apart, pinning her arms to her sides. She doesn't fight me. Giving her one last burning look, I lower my head and draw my tongue through her pink slit.

One taste is all it takes for me to forget the vicious ache of my cock.

Fuck. She tastes incredible, better than I imagined, and I get to work, doing my best of lick and suck her clean. It's a fool's errand. Within seconds, more wetness is flowing over my tongue and shy little cries above my head are getting louder. She's not holding back anymore, and it's not an exaggeration to say I could do this all fucking night.

I'm consumed by the effect I'm having on her. Every little shake, every whine, every gasp, is filed away for future reference.

She's barely a woman and has only just started to understand her body and explore what it needs. It's not good enough to make her come. Any fucker with half a brain can bring a woman to orgasm if he cares enough to. If this is all I have of her, if this one night is all I get, then I need to make sure she never forgets me.

I want her to think about me when she lays alone at night, fingers in her needy pussy.

I want her to think about me when there's another man balls-deep inside her, taking what should have been mine.

I want to imprint myself on her, to weave myself into the fabric of her body and her soul.

Keeping her isn't an option, but—as tonight has incontrovertibly proven—I'm selfish.

Already her cunt is swollen and sensitive, but I'm not going easy. Adina's body is shaking now, her legs falling open wider, and the sweet essence of her arousal is flowing freely over my tongue. I'm doing this to her. *Me.*

My left hand comes up to grip the back of her knee, pushing forward so I have room to plunge my tongue into that needy little hole. From this angle, I have the perfect view of her perky tits, and my cock leaps when I watch her hands move to twist and pull at her own nipples. She apparently likes a little pain with her pleasure. *Noted.*

Unable to help myself, my free hand finds my engorged dick, squeezing myself to the point of pain. It doesn't help —nothing fucking helps—because I am fucking a gorgeous twenty-one-year-old with my tongue, and she's practically writhing from the pleasure I'm giving her. This is the most erotic moment of my life, nothing will ever compare to this, and even the slightest friction would likely make me blow.

Fuck it.

My hand begins to move up and down my shaft in vicious strokes. Desperate for her to come, I move my tongue over her clit in flat, hard strokes. Seconds later, her body goes rigid. This orgasm is different than earlier. She comes and comes, and while there are no moans of "daddy" or loud cries, I can tell this is more intense. She needed this, needed me on my knees with my tongue in her beautiful, little pussy.

I come seconds later, still trying to soothe her swollen clit with my tongue, even as my body shakes with the force of how hard I'm coming and my release covers my own hand. *Fuck.* I fall forward, pressing my face into her lower stomach, panting and breathing her in.

I don't need to try to remember any of this, though. For how determined I've been to ensure she's never free of me, I somehow failed to recognize that I wouldn't be free either.

When I finally have the strength to lift my head and lean back, Adina follows me. Her warm hands find my face, and then she's kissing me again. Not with the wild desperation of earlier, but tender and slow. Being kissed like this feels like someone has taken a knife to my chest and cut me open. There's nowhere to hide, and I couldn't resist if I tried.

The bedroom is through the door behind us, and I pull back only so I can get to my feet and hurry across the room to wipe my cum on the abandoned towel. When I turn back to her, I find Adina watching me, leaning back on her elbows with the city sparkling through the window behind her. She looks exhausted.

Something inside me pulls taught, tugging me back to her, and I don't fight it. I cross the room to lift her into my arms, loving the way she twines her arms around my neck and the warm weight of her naked body against mine.

"Stay here tonight," I plead.

I am not ready for this to be over. How could I possibly watch her walk out the door and into the cold night, knowing it will be the last time I ever see her? Even Adina's quiet acceptance does nothing to soothe the vicious point of pain that's appeared in the center of my chest. Even if it's not now, I'll still have to say goodbye soon. Reminding myself that this is my own doing, that it's better this way, only makes the pain sharpen as I lay her back on the bed.

She moves over, and, like we've done this a thousand times before, I follow. We don't speak as I pull the covers over us both and curl my body around hers.

Adina's fingers dance over mine. "Tell me a secret."

Her voice is sleepy, and my answering laugh ghosts over the bare skin of her shoulder. "What kind of secret?"

She hums, her hand drifting to play with the hair dusting my forearm. "Any kind."

I want you for more than tonight.

The room is dark. Even the city's light is blocked out by the heavy, rich drapes covering the windows. I close my eyes, breathing her in, savoring every little brush of skin and the feeling of her back rising and falling steadily against my chest. It's strange to be utterly content while still dreading something so deeply.

"My mother lives in Florida. I went to visit her for the holidays this year."

"Why is that a secret?"

"It isn't." My throat is tight. Of all the things I could have told her—sordid events from college, things that make me look interesting or funny or cool—this is what I choose? "It's that I didn't have anyone to pick me up from the airport."

A second passes, then two. I'm scrambling for some way to laugh this off, to play it off as nothing, when Adina moves. Turning over in my arms, her hands cradling my face in the darkness. I realize too late that my eyes are wet. When was the last time I cried? Christ—I can't remember. Lindsey leaving was the biggest, supposedly devastating moment of my life, and I didn't shed a tear. Even sitting in that airplane, hollowed out with loneliness, I kept myself together.

I don't have time to be embarrassed, though, because there's a quiet sniffle through the darkness.

"Sorry." Adina laughs sadly. "That hit close to home."

"Angel—"

"No! It's okay!" She nestles a little closer, her soft legs brushing against mine. "Things are okay for me now, but I get it. That feeling. I'm so sorry, Asher."

Not as sorry as I am. I would take feeling that way

forever if it meant she never again experienced that gaping chasm inside her. Everything about this woman is *good*. She deserves to be cherished. She deserves everything.

I have no right, none at all, but—fuck me—I want to give it to her.

eight

ADINA

TIME'S UP.

I knew this was coming, obviously, but my heart still feels heavy as I slide out of the warm hotel bed. Asher is still sprawled out on his stomach, sound asleep, and his heavy breathing is the only noise in the room apart from the muffled sound of traffic eight floors below us. There's a pleasant soreness between my legs, a reminder of the three —no, four? Who knows how many—orgasms he wrung from my body before I fell asleep in his arms.

Sleeping beside someone was yet another first for me. I didn't set my alarm. For once, though, the constant, gnawing exhaustion that usually plagues me is nowhere to be found.

Last night wasn't what I expected it to be. I all but offered myself to Asher Roth on a silver platter, fully prepared to lose my virginity to him, and he chose to spend our first and only night together entirely focused on making *me* feel good. Granted, my experience with one-night stands is pretty limited, but I do know that sex is usually involved.

Exhaling raggedly, I scan the spotless room, which looks so much fancier during the day than it did last night. At some point while I was sleeping, Asher must have gone out into the living room to clean up, because my clothes are folded neatly on the chair beside the door with the new purse from Ruby resting on top.

My throat tightens as I stare at the pile. There's no reason to read into it. He was probably trying to be nice.

One night. He made it perfectly clear that this wasn't going to be repeated, and I agreed. We didn't discuss the particulars, but even someone like me knows the rules here: you have sex, you sleep, and then you go home. While there *wasn't* sex, and there *was* a weirdly intense, emotional moment in there as well, I'm pretty sure the last part is still applicable. Undoubtedly, he doesn't want me to hang around his super expensive hotel suite or read into things.

A quick peek at the clock on my phone confirms that I slept way longer than my designated four hours, and I need to be at work soon. I couldn't stay, even if I wanted to. Which I don't. Casual is exactly what I needed. We had fun, but I can now resume my regularly scheduled life with one mind-blowing sexual experience and three thousand extra dollars under my belt.

Which *doesn't* make me a prostitute. I was paid to have dinner with him, *which I did*, and then I left. Everything after that was all me.

I'm careful to close the bathroom door extra quietly so it doesn't wake Ash. *Wow.* The room is floor-to-ceiling marble, and the tile is warm beneath my bare feet. On the counter, I find a whole array of complimentary toiletries and eagerly help myself to one of the biodegradable bamboo toothbrushes, plus some lotion that smells like rich people.

Staring at my reflection in the mirror above the sink, I can't help twisting a little, examining my naked body from every angle. Apart from a few bruises on my breasts, which I'm positive are from Ash's mouth, there's no sign of what we spent last night doing. I *feel* different, though—sexy, grown up, and confident, all except the question gnawing at me since I woke up.

Why didn't he want to have sex with me? Was it because —Nope. I shake myself mentally. Not going there.

It's tempting to stay a while longer, if only to take advantage of the enormous glass-enclosed shower or test out all the different kinds of bubble bath resting along the edge of the tub. Real life is calling, though, and I know I need to get back up town to change before work. Maybe, if I'm an extra good person for the next however many years, I can haunt this bathroom when I die. I'd deal with all the naked rich people if it meant I could spend my afterlife using that bathtub.

Giving myself one last once-over in the floor-length mirror on the back of the door, I push my hair behind my ears and open the door just wide enough to peek out cautiously.

Asher is still sleeping, spread out on his stomach beneath the white bedding, the top half of his surprisingly muscular back visible. One arm is stretched out to where I'd been laying beside him only moments ago, like he was unconsciously reaching for me.

Catching my bottom lip between my teeth, I pause. The urge to call in to work for the first time ever and stay with him is so strong, it's like a physical ache.

There's no point in drawing this out.

Even with the extra three grand in my bank account, I can't stomach passing up a whole eight-hour shift. Especially when the man I want to crawl back into bed and cuddle with left my clothes by the door.

It's better like this, to go without the awkwardness. What would he even say if I woke him up to say goodbye?

Thanks for everything?

I had fun eating your pussy, have a nice life?

My soul shrivels at the thought. Nope. Better to slip out of here with my dignity intact and my last memory of Asher being his low, rough voice in my ear, waking me up and ordering me to come on his fingers sometime in the early hours of the morning. Will the letters he leaves for Allison hurt for a while? Probably. I signed up for this, though. I knew what I was getting myself into, and now it's time to face reality.

Shoving aside the impulse to get back into bed, I cross to the pile of my things.

I'm just pulling my thong back over my hips when I hear a soft rustle of bedding behind me, and my heart leaps into my throat. I spin around to find Asher sitting up, looking at me through bleary eyes, his hair flat on one side and sticking up on the other.

Something inside me twists painfully. I'm so into him. I can't lie to myself.

"Come back to bed." His voice is still rough with sleep, and he has to fumble blindly on the bedside table for a few seconds to find his glasses.

I want to. More than anything I want to. If this is hard now… I shake my head. It seems to take a lot more effort to smile than it usually does. "I have to go. Work in a few hours."

Be cool, Adina.

Asher falls silent as I turn my attention to my dress, wincing at the state of it. My one saving grace is that, by some miracle, Doctor Roth's office will be closed for the first Saturday since I started working there, probably because the man himself wanted to go downtown and have unattached sex. He got what he wanted—kind of—and now I thankfully won't have to wait until tonight to change my clothes. None of my coworkers have ever come in for a shift wearing a wrinkled designer cocktail dress that shows half their boobs, and I don't want to be the first.

"Wait a moment."

I don't dare look up as Asher moves around the other side of the bed. My whole face is burning, and I hold the dress to my front, covering myself the best I can. Last night, he saw every inch of my body, and touched most of it. But it's different in the light of day, when the amount of time we have left together can be measured in minutes.

A second later, Asher is at my side, holding out a pair of sweatpants and white T-shirt.

"Thank you." I take the clothes and pull them on quickly as he moves past me to sit at the edge of the bed, silently watching as I dress. The weight of his gaze is impossible to ignore, but I do my best. The T-shirt falls to mid-thigh, and the sweatpants are so big I have to roll them up four times, but it's better than the walk-of-shame ensemble.

What is he thinking right now? Is he relieved I'm not a desperate virgin, trying to draw this out? I bet that's why he didn't sleep with me. Too much baggage. Fair enough.

He's quiet as I gather my things, and I'm wishing I *didn't* want him to say something. Why can't I be one of those women who is capable of having a fun, sexy hookup and then going on her way with a smile? Ruby does it all the time, and jokes later about their penis size or the weird stuff in their bathroom cabinet. That's how it's supposed to be. I'm twenty-one years old; I should be out there looking for a good time, not throwing myself at the one man in this city I have feelings for.

Every second that passes without him saying anything hurts more.

I can't lie to myself anymore, and I can't delay the inevitable. I have no more reason to be here, and he clearly doesn't care. I'd known it was the end when I woke up, but this is *really* the end.

My heart is lodged in my throat as I cast one last look around the room to make sure I haven't forgotten anything, carefully avoiding looking directly at Asher. My poker face is usually foolproof but right now, when I'm feeling all these big, conflicting emotions, I'm not sure I can pull it off.

I swallow, attempting a cheerful, casual tone as I stare at the doorknob. "Well. Thanks for dinner."

"Adina." There's a quiet command in his voice, and I can't resist obeying.

Reluctantly, I turn to face him. "It was fun. The food and the, um, orgasms? Thank you for that." I wince. God, could I sound any more awkward right now?

Asher chuckles quietly. "Come here." He reaches for me, and like my body has a mind of its own, I draw closer to him. The moment I'm within reach, his hands find my waist and he tugs me forward so I'm standing between his legs, staring down into his bright-blue eyes.

He's silent for a long time, looking conflicted. Finally, he speaks in a quiet rush, "I'm going to be back here next weekend. Would you consider meeting me here?"

My pulse throbs, and my stomach knots as his words sink in. Looking down at him, Asher looks... vulnerable, actually. Dressed in only boxers and glasses, he gazes up at me apprehensively. Understanding washes over me, and suddenly, I want to laugh. He's worried that *I'm* going to say no, that *I'm* going to want to stick to the one-night-only agreement.

Unable to help myself, I reach forward, weaving my fingers into his messy hair. My thumbs find his temples and I press slightly, massaging until the tension bleeds from his shoulders and his eyes drop shut. The quiet groan that rumbles from his chest makes the tender muscles between my thighs tense.

Holy crap, this is actually happening. *He wants me.*

"If you could stop being so hot for two minutes, that would help me think a little more clearly."

Ash's eyes snap open, eyebrows lifting in disbelief at my comment. "I think if either one of us is punching above our weight class, it's me." He smiles wryly, and there's only one way I can respond to that. My heart throbs as I lean down to kiss him softly.

It's perfect. Slow and familiar, as that little ember of hope that was all but dead only a few minutes ago begins to grow, warming me all over. He had his head between my legs less than twelve hours ago. I thought I knew just how good this man could make me feel, but this is so much better.

Asher's arms wind around me, pulling me close, and I melt. I'm pretty sure I would be a puddle on the ground if he weren't holding me up.

Oh, fuck. Yes. Definitely so much better.

The way he tastes, the warmth of his almost naked body seeping through the borrowed clothes into my own, and the knowledge this isn't the last time I'll see him...

I pull away, stepping back toward the door before I throw caution to the wind, call out sick, and spend the whole day in Asher's arms. My heart swells at the way he leans forward, like he's resisting the urge to follow. "Next Friday?" I confirm, my face splitting in a huge smile.

He nods, his throat bobbing. "I'll leave a key at the desk for you."

Okay, then.

My heart feels about twenty times lighter than it did when I woke up as I gather the last of my things and my hand finds the door handle behind me. I push it open, backing out into the living room. "See you Friday, then, Mr. Roth."

Doctor Roth,
I got the bathrooms painted (as you can hopefully tell). I hope you had a good weekend.

-A

Allison,
I had an excellent weekend, actually. The best I've had in ages. I left the extra money (as you can hopefully tell) for painting. Is it enough to cover books and supplies? You have another year of school to go, right? Maybe we can work something out over summer break to get you some extra work. Let me know if you're interested!
-Doctor Roth

I'M ANNOYED, but not surprised, to find Liam Witt sitting in procedure room two.

It's the Monday following my weekend at The Witt, and I'm just returning from lunch. Upon entering the building, I found my dental assistants being much more giggly than usual, and a (mostly eaten) box of gourmet pastries from a downtown bakery on the reception desk. Having been friends with the man for the better part of twenty years, I'm familiar with Liam's tactics for charming groups of women.

Sure enough, my friend/the living poltergeist is grinning proudly up at me from the exam chair when I walk into the room instead of the six-year-old I was expecting to encounter.

Sighing in resignation, I drop the chart on the counter and snatch a pair of gloves from the holder. If he's here, he can at least get a checkup. Somehow, I doubt Liam is keeping up on his regular preventative healthcare. Snapping them on, I glare at him. "What are you doing here?"

Liam shrugs, leaning back without complaint as I press

the button to drop the chair. "I was in the neighborhood. I didn't hear from you after Friday."

"I've been busy." I turn on the overhead light and pull it into place, trying not to feel defensive. I didn't do anything wrong. Liam fucks his way through a good chunk of Manhattan's population—male and female—every fiscal quarter.

My spending the night with one woman isn't going to shock him. What might is that we didn't have sex, yet I've still been replaying our night together on repeat since I left The Witt.

Meeting her was, without question, the most intense night of my life, and I still haven't recovered from it.

For fuck's sake, my right arm aches now because I've been jerking off to the memories of it with all the frequency and enthusiasm of a pre-teen boy who just discovered porn.

It's hard to remember what branch of convoluted logic I employed to convince myself that one night with Adina was enough. Whatever it was, it's clear I was testing the limits of my own self-control and resolve, and it all came crumbling down the moment I woke up and saw how close I came to sleeping through those last minutes with her. The terror and regret that filled me in that moment confirmed what I'd instinctively known from the very first time I saw her across the lounge: *I need more.*

Not just more of her body—though that was certainly enough to alter my brain's chemistry until the end of time —but more of *her*. I want her bright smiles, her laugh, her warmth and kindness. I want to make her laugh, to feed her things she's never tried and see her eyes light up when she tastes something she loves. And, most terrifying of all, I want to *take care of her.*

Instincts and desires I didn't think I was capable of are

roaring to life, shining a stark, unflattering light over my previous relationship by comparison.

Watching as I open the instrument pack, Liam hums thoughtfully. "You never told me what happened with Ruby's friend. Adele?"

"Adina," I correct him, a little too fast.

Liam's eyes gleam. "*Adina.* I apologize. It's an unusual name. Almost as unusual as you enjoying yourself, which you certainly seemed to be doing on Friday."

I swallow the tightness in my throat. "Open." He obeys, and I buy myself a few minutes by running through a basic exam, pretending to be engrossed in the state of my oldest friend's teeth instead of scrambling for what I should or shouldn't tell him. When I can't put it off any longer, I clear my throat, setting the used instruments back on the tray table. "I liked her."

"Interesting."

That's all I get. *Interesting.*

"We didn't have"—I drop my voice on the off chance a child happens to be walking past the room—"*sex.*"

I sound like an eighth-grade boy, and can't really blame Liam for laughing at me. Swinging his legs over the side of the chair, he sits up without waiting for me to lift the back. "I'd have been jealous if you did. She was certainly... attractive. Not my usual type, but a change would do me good. Perhaps I'll have Ruby arrange a night with just the three of us. I'd love to get to know her better." Despite the relatively tame words, his tone all but drips with suggestion.

Evidently, knowing I'm being bated does nothing to prevent me from biting. Gritting my teeth, I rip my gloves off and get to my feet. "You have some gum recession. Go see your dentist if you don't want to be eating your dinner through a straw in twenty years."

Liam doesn't seem the least bit bothered about his dental troubles. His smile widens. "I won't go out with her if you ask me not to. I'm an excellent friend like that."

"You're a hedonistic chimpanzee with a bottomless bank account." I turn to go, but a sick feeling of dread writhes inside me. I pause, holding the door frame, and glance over my shoulder at Liam. He's still watching me from his place on the chair, smugger than ever. As little as I want to give him the satisfaction, I want to worry about him fucking Adina even less. Which means it's time to swallow my pride.

"Was there something else?" His eyes shine with the anticipation of victory.

I hate him so much.

Making a mental note to find out how adult men make new friends, I blow out a furious breath. "Please don't go out with her."

Liam hums. "I never took you for the jealous type."

"You—"

He sighs dramatically, as if I'm being a pain in the ass and gaining a brand-new source of leverage over me won't be the highlight of his whole month. "She wouldn't have agreed, anyway."

I was in the process of mentally composing a more elegant insult when I falter, staring at him. "What does that mean?"

Without another word, Liam reaches into his pocket and takes out his phone. He pulls something up on the screen and holds it out for me to take, eyes sparkling. "It *means* that I don't think she's in it for the money."

Swallowing, I stare down at what appears to be a transaction on a payment-processing app.

· · ·

Payment to Adina Collier (January 20): $3,000.00

Payment from Adina Collier (January 21): $3,000.000

She returned the money?

I exhale heavily, head spinning as I hand the phone back.

"I must say," Liam drawls as he stands, brushing non-existent creases from the sleeves of his shirt. "I've never had a woman refuse to take money from me before. Are you going to see her again?"

Mutely, I nod, watching him cross to the corner to retrieve his coat from the cartoon whale-shaped hook.

She turned down the money.

Holy shit.

It hadn't even occurred to me to hope for this. After all, three thousand dollars must have seemed like a miracle for a broke college student with two jobs. Her turning it down means that she valued me—*us*—over financial stability.

All my instincts about Adina were right. She's incredible, the kind of woman you bend over backwards to keep, and I reduced her to a one-night stand. *I fucking lied to her.*

Through the end of my relationship with Lindsey, it somehow never crossed my mind that maybe the reason I couldn't commit was because a part of me knew we were *wrong*. It's a dangerous train of thought, one that means accepting the possibility that the too beautiful, too kind, too young, and utterly wrong for me Adina, could be *right*.

Which is—obviously—a completely insane thing to consider about a woman you barely know.

Liam pauses beside me on his way to the door, and I

start, so lost in my own head that I'd somehow forgotten he was here.

"I know we don't say shit like this because we're emotionally stunted men with some fairly obvious abandonment issues"—his hand finds my shoulder, and he grips it bracingly—"but for the record, you're a good person, Ash. Great, even. You deserve to be happy."

My chest is tight as I nod jerkily, staring at the floor. "Thank you."

He's right, we don't say shit like this, but now that we are... I look up to find his expression is uncharacteristically grave. "For the record, you're a good person too, Liam. Obnoxious"—I smile wryly—"but good. You deserve more than people who are only interested in your money."

My best friend of two decades grins and lets his hand fall, already moving toward the door. "That's what I have you for, Roth."

ADINA

THE SLEEP SITUATION is getting out of hand. Not only have I increased my allotted sleep time to six hours, I'm drinking so much coffee that my heart has begun doing this (probably bad) fluttering thing, and I'm *still* exhausted.

I know the whole medical community seems to be in agreement about the whole eight-hour thing, but obviously none of them have been a homeless college student trying to break out of her family's cycle of generational poverty, mental illness, and addiction. I can't get eight hours. I just can't.

Further complicating matters is the dreams.

Not nightmares—fairly surprising given my personal history. *Nope.* My subconscious isn't interested in reliving trauma or manifesting deep-seeded fears. Every night, no matter how dead tired I am, I dream about being fucked by Asher Roth.

Sometimes the dreams are hazy and slow, a man's hands roaming over my body, leaving prickly heat in their wake. Other times it's so real and vivid that I get swept away, only to wake up panting and hollow with my panties drenched.

It's a problem. *A real freakin' problem.* If I were really so tired, it seems pretty counterintuitive for my brain to be drumming up sex dreams instead of resting. Unless this is all some biological clock thing, in which case it can chill, because I'm twenty-one. Also, the Collier family tree hasn't exactly produced a lot of stable, undamaged fruit as far as I'm aware, so maybe I'd be better off adopting.

Come to think of it, the fact that my brain is using precious energy to tell me to get laid rather than function at maximum capacity is pretty convincing evidence that this particular branch of the evolutionary tree needs to end with me.

It's been four days since I left The Witt, and so far, I've managed to avoid Ruby. We have classes together, but I'm always hurrying off somewhere afterward, and she hasn't had the opportunity to corner me. There's no way around it now, though. We have a presentation for our ethics class first thing tomorrow morning, and she's my partner.

I feel like I'm marching to the principal's office, a red-hot ball of dread sitting in the pit of my stomach and a certainty I'm about to get a proper scolding. Ruby isn't one to mince words, and she certainly wouldn't approve of me meeting Asher again. Or of the not so insignificant fact that I returned the three thousand dollar "gift" from Liam Witt, which appeared in my Cashed app halfway through my shift at the coffee shop on Saturday.

That's the part that would send up about a hundred red flags for Ruby, because who in their right mind would turn down three thousand dollars? She doesn't even know that I sleep on a dentist's couch every night and shower at a fitness center, but she'd still be appalled. Hell, I'm a little appalled at myself. That money would have been a godsend, yet every time I opened the app, convinced I was going to hit that glowing green ACCEPT button, I just felt sick and small.

Asher Roth saved my life; he's the only person in the world who could connect the person I was then to whom I've worked so hard to make myself become. I couldn't live with myself if he ever found out his friend paid me to act interested in him. I wasn't acting, so I didn't deserve that money. Simple(ish).

Not that I can explain any of that to Ruby Johnson.

The woman is *scary*. She can detect bullshit with all the accuracy of a bomb-sniffing dog and has made it no secret she finds my lack of personal life boring as hell. The events of Friday are unprecedented, and undoubtedly she's been waiting to get me alone and find out what happened. I'm not excited about trying to pass this whole business with Asher off as nothing, and I have no idea how I could tell her the truth without divulging a whole lot more of my shitty life than I want to.

Sure enough, when I get to the library, Ruby's bright eyes are like twin lasers, boring into me as I wind my way through the maze of study tables. "Well, well, well," she says, barely able to contain her glee as I slide into the seat across from her.

Even the way she closes her laptop is smug.

Valiantly attempting to ignore her and pretend my face *isn't* red as a tomato right now, I focus on pulling out my battered computer and English textbook.

When I've successfully located a plug for my charger and there's nothing left to do, I'm forced to peek up at her. "Good morning."

In response, Ruby cackles so loudly it attracts disparaging looks from the girls at the next table.

Ignoring them, she leans forward, lowering her voice. "For *you*, I bet. The last time I saw you, I had to practically drag you into that hotel. You can imagine my surprise when I find you practically drooling all over Liam's friend. We went back to the lounge after dinner, you know, and neither of you were *anywhere* to be found."

My cheeks get hotter somehow. "I liked him," I admit, dropping my eyes to my computer screen to avoid looking at her directly.

Ruby scoffs. "Understatement. You guys were *so cute*. I've never seen you take to anyone like that." She lowers her voice, excitement coloring her tone. "Did you guys come to an... *arrangement?*"

I know exactly what kind of arrangement she's talking about. Just like that, my mood sours.

"It's not like that." I flip open my book, thumbing through chapters to get to the one we need. "I... really did like him."

Too much. I'm in way further than I should be given that I have absolutely no proof Asher isn't just in this for fun. My *brain* totally gets it, but my traitorous heart is already whispering *what if* in between sending up elaborate fantasies of wedding dresses and family vacations.

Stupid.

Despite this wildly improbable turn of events and my subsequent night as horny Cinderella, my life isn't a fairy tale. It doesn't seem to matter how many times I tell myself that, however. I can't seem to snuff out the little ember of hope that's now burning away in my heart.

Ruby's right. I'm okay with being polite, or even kind. When it comes to really connecting, though? No way. I'm out. I began construction on the twenty-foot-tall, barbed-wire-topped wall around myself before I was even out of grade school. It's still there now, heavily fortified and standing ready to keep out any and all intruders who might get in the way of my escaping my shitty origins.

No friends. No lovers. Nobody who might ask too many questions or get too close.

I let Asher in, though. He's been inside for years now, claiming my heart with every stupid knock-knock joke left on a Post-it note and his utterly unselfish support. Taking the proverbial plunge and being brave was easy with him, because I'd already done it. It's the other stuff, the uncertainty and the lies and the money, that are harder.

Hard or not, though, I still spend my sleeping hours dreaming about his hands on me and my waking hours remembering how I can't stop thinking about how good it felt to fall asleep in his arms or to wake up beside him. There was something so *natural* about it—even if I knew it wouldn't happen again. It felt like we'd done it a thousand times.

He said it was just for one night, but he asked me to meet him next weekend too. Was it just that he wasn't sure if he would like me enough to commit to another "date," or did he feel just a tiny bit of the clawing panic I did when I thought I would never see him like that again? Is he panicking about his lie, just like I'm panicking about mine?

I'm so mixed up and confused, I don't know which way to spin out first.

"Adina. I like Liam too." There's sympathy and warning in Ruby's voice that's like a bucket of water thrown over the hope kindling in my chest. She doesn't need to say anything else. I get it. She likes Liam, but she doesn't expect more from him than he's offered her. Her heart is her own.

We might not be friends, exactly, but Ruby is looking out for me. She can tell I'm in danger of making the oldest mistake known to womankind: falling for the wrong man.

Hitching an unconvincing smile on my face, I finally manage to look up to meet her penetrating gaze across the table. "I'm okay. Seriously. It's nothing. I'll probably never see him again."

Liar.

I turn my eyes back to my computer, trying to ignore the weight that has suddenly settled inside me.

If there's one thing my mother taught me, it's that relationships come and go. I need to take care of myself and build a future that nobody else can take from me. This money would have brought me just a little bit closer to the stability I've been craving my whole life, yet I didn't take it because I want Asher Roth to *like me?*

Ruby leans forward, her lips pursed. "Just keep your shit together. Guys like Liam and Asher only want us for one thing, and feelings aren't required."

eleven

ASHER

UNLIKE MY VISIT to The Witt last week, there isn't a personal concierge waiting to take my bags or offer me complimentary use of any of the hotel's many amenities; I'm not a personal guest of the owner this time. While the distinction certainly comes with its perks, I'm grateful to be able to escape up to my room without questions from Liam.

I'm in no shape to make polite conversation with anyone. With every day that's brought me closer to Friday, I've become more and more distracted, struggling to think about anything other than *her*. Depending on the hour, I swing wildly between guilt and restless excitement.

Giving her four orgasms and taking none for myself assuaged some of the burning guilt for my lies. *Some.* Not all, because god knows feeling Adina's body writhing against mine, hearing her call me *daddy* as she came apart on my mouth, fingers, and cock... I'll be getting off to memories of that night for the rest of my life.

There was nothing altruistic about it.

Then, learning she turned down the money—*for me?* The woman is a college student working two jobs, she obviously needed it. I may be a selfish bastard, but I can't stomach taking anything from her when she doesn't know the truth about me.

When Adina comes—*no*—if. *If Adina comes.* We didn't exactly leave things on solid ground. I could tell she was unsure. How could she not be when I changed the boundaries of our relationship at the last possible moment? The boundaries *I'd* set. There's a very good chance that she won't show tonight. If she doesn't, will I be able to let this go?

My pride says *yes.*

The rest of me says *no.*

The room I'm in is considerably smaller than the suite Liam gave me last time, with just a small living area and massive bed. I'm avoiding looking at it because my cock throbs every time I catch sight of the carefully ironed white bedding, hopeful fantasies of what it will look like in a few hours blooming in my imagination.

As if all this wasn't excruciatingly embarrassing enough, there's also a selection of bags from my favorite take-out restaurants in the city arranged on the small, round table in the corner. I've been so fidgety since getting here, I took them out of the bags and then put them back in about four times. Was I showing my hand? Trying too hard? Not trying hard enough?

I'm about to begin my fifth cycle of taking the food out of the bags when there's a quiet knock on the door, and it's like someone has flipped a switch inside me. My whole body is suddenly on edge, and in five paces I've crossed the room—all while convincing myself it's only someone with the wrong room—and pulled open the door.

Heat surges up my spine, and my head spins. I hadn't allowed myself to actually believe she'd come. But here she is, gazing up at me through wide, green eyes, her lips curled into a shy smile.

Adina.

The last time I saw her, she was swathed in my over-sized clothing, and before that it was a cocktail dress obviously chosen to impress. Now—adorable and comfortable in jeans and a sweater, her braided hair sticking out from beneath a white knit cap—now is better. She looks very much like the college girl I can't bring myself to regret she is.

Jesus Christ, she's so sweet.

"Hi," Adina breathes, curling her hand around the strap of an overstuffed backpack slung over one shoulder. Her smile becomes a little sheepish as it hits me what's inside.

She brought a change of clothes.

"Hi," I echo, my throat working as I step back, allowing her past me into the room.

Miraculously, she's even more beautiful than I remember, her eyes scanning the smaller room without a hint of disappointment that it isn't a massive suite. She stills when she sees the take-out bags on the table, and my heart flips at the smile that spreads over her face.

"You didn't have to do all this for me." She turns, her eyes wide with undisguised shock.

As thrilled as I am to have made her happy, it pisses me the fuck off that a woman this incredible doesn't expect to be treated like a princess. She deserves it—more than deserves it—and my initial shock at her appearance has been washed away by fury with every single person in Adina's life who managed to miss the mark so spectacularly.

"Yes. I did," I say shortly, reaching out to take her bag. The back of my hand brushes her neck in the process, and even that tiny contact sends electricity up my arm. We both stiffen, staring at each other.

Slowly, like she's expecting me to back away, Adina closes the distance between us. I stand stock-still, stomach knotting as she pushes onto her toes and leaves the shortest, sweetest kiss on the corner of my mouth. It's chaste, barely a kiss at all, but that's all it takes.

I'm ruined.

I know, right then and there, that I'm going to fight for this woman. Even if it makes me selfish. Even if she'd be better off with someone her own age. I may not have as much to offer as a man like Liam, but what I do have is hers. One day, my kids are going to ask me when I knew their mom was the one, and this is the moment I'll remember.

I realize I've been frozen, staring at her as the force of this realization rushes over me. Adina bites her lip, eyebrows lifting in worry. "I'm sorry, I—"

She doesn't get to finish the thought. Seconds later, my body is pressing hers into the wall, and her gasp of surprise is silenced by my kiss. Fuck. The taste of her hits me all over again. I groan, the tips of my fingers pushing into her hair as my hands cradle her face. Adina's hands tighten on my shirt, relax, and tighten again, as though she's trying to keep herself in check and failing miserably.

It's not messy or rough, unhurried by the fierce urgency of the last time we were together, because this will not be the last time I kiss this woman. Still, every ragged breath, every brush of her tongue against mine, throws fuel on the need burning inside me. I want her. I want her so fucking much it feels like I might break apart if I don't get inside her.

I need to come clean about my job and where I live. I need to confess that Liam was trying to make me sound far more impressive than I really am, and I'm not sure when the right time to do that is. Things are so fragile now—so *new*. She's still nervous around me and, like it or not, I don't know what her true motives are for being here. She may want me—at least in part—for the stability she thinks I can provide. This whole situation has become a tangled minefield, and I have no idea how to navigate it without shattering her trust in me forever or sending her running for the hills.

Pulling back, I press my forehead against hers. "Adina." I love calling her angel, but saying her name is so much better. I love that she's the only woman I've ever known who has it. Already it feels so familiar, like I've been saying it all my life instead of a few days, as easy and as comfortable as telling someone the name of my hometown. Panting, she gazes back at me, and again I'm struck by that feeling of rightness.

"Sorry." She laughs breathlessly. "I just…"

She doesn't need to say the words for me to know what they were. My girl missed me, and she thinks telling me that will scare me off, and I fucking *hate* it. That's not the kind of relationship I want with her. I won't have her holding back or pretending. I want to know exactly who she is and fall for every last personality quirk, even the ones that drive me insane.

I can't blame her. This is my fault. If I hadn't been such a tangled mess the night we met, things would have been different. Now, she has no idea what I want from her, and it's my job to make sure she doesn't leave this hotel without clearing up at least some of the mess I made.

"I missed you this week." My fingers find a stray lock of hair and tuck it behind her ear, taking care to let my hand brush over the delicate skin of her neck. Adina melts against me, and her answering smile is so big and unrestrained, it makes something in my chest pull taught. "Come here." Reluctantly, I pull back and take her hand in mine, pulling her over to the table.

She takes the seat across from mine and looks around at the selection I brought, unable to hide her enthusiasm as I begin opening dishes. "Thank you *so much*, Asher. This all looks incredible. The only thing I've eaten all day is stale donuts in the break room at my internship."

"Of course." I pause, watching her help herself to Chinese food. "Can I ask where you're interning?"

Adina's eyes flash up to mine, and I can tell she's surprised to find me watching her so intently. "Oh! Sure. It's not a secret or anything. I'm at the Department of Child Welfare. Mostly it's administrative stuff, but today I got to go with my supervisor to complete some home visits approving new foster families." Her enthusiasm is obvious, as if most twenty-one-year-olds wouldn't rather be doing anything else, and suddenly, it hits me how wrong I was about this.

How could I have been so foolish as to think she was in this for the money when every action she's taken thus far has proven the opposite?

"I have a confession to make." I swallow the lump in my throat, my chest tight with anxiety. "My ex-girlfriend and I were together for six years, and we just broke up a few months ago. I haven't... dated since then."

Adina's face has grown pale and, slowly, she sets down her fork beside her plate. Her hands drop into her lap. "You want something casual. I understand. I didn't assume anything coming here again—"

My stomach plummets. "No! *Oh fuck*—absolutely not." It's an intense response, but I can't help it. *Casual?* I rake a hand through my hair, staring at her as I struggle to find the right words. "The opposite, actually. I like you. Very much. I don't want to fuck this up. Last week, what Liam told you about me wasn't the truth. He was trying to get me back out there..." I trail off miserably. "I'm a dentist. I own a practice in Harlem. It's—*ah*—aggressively unprofitable. I'm sorry. I know this is a lot to throw at you on the second date. It's just that I like you, and I'd like to keep seeing you."

Across from me, Adina is still, and there's something else in her expression now that I can't quite identify. Finally, she nods slightly. "I'd like to keep seeing you too."

"That's it?" I chuckle, but it sounds hollow. "You don't want to get out while you still can? There's still time—*Shit*. Please ignore me. I'm a terrible salesman." What the hell is wrong with me? I'm trying to win her over, not show her the door.

Adina's lips press together, like she's trying to stop herself from laughing. "You don't need to sell me on yourself, Asher Roth. I haven't been able to stop thinking about you. I just..." Her eyes search my face, the ghost of her smile fading. "My past is complicated. I did things I'm not proud of, things I'm ashamed of. It's not easy for me to talk about it."

Fuck, she's killing me right now. "You don't have to. Not until you're ready." I reach my hand out over the table, palm up, and Adina's eyes swim with tears as she takes it. "When you are, though, I'm here. You can trust me."

Her answering smile is sad. "I know."

twelve

ADINA

"I CAN'T!"

Asher's fingers dig into my hips, and he gives an impatient little growl. "Sit on my fucking face, Adina."

I squirm, trying to ignore the effect this command has on me, but I'm fighting a losing battle. My hands are planted between my spread thighs on Asher's bare shoulders, holding myself back as he tries to tug me forward. "You're going to suffocate," I protest weakly, well aware my pussy has a mind of its own. Heat spreads out from my throbbing clit, and I'm pretty sure the muscles in my legs are trying to stage an outright rebellion and collapse out from under me, but I still don't move.

He made me eat first, even after the make-out session that followed his confession. I like him so much, *more* than like him, but I feel so guilty. Asher Roth wants me. He isn't playing around or in this for easy sex. Whatever I told myself before, I hoped desperately this was the case. Now that it is, I'm so woefully unprepared. After all, he's being honest with me, he's trying to show me I can trust him and that he cares enough to make himself vulnerable. He's perfect—the most amazing person I've ever known and my own personal hero—and he doesn't even know it.

My own personal hero, who now wants me to sit on his face and possibly smother him with my pussy.

A hand comes down on my ass in a sharp swat, and I gasp, looking down at Asher. He took off his glasses as we stumbled over to the bed, shedding clothes and touching each other in between searing, hungry kisses.

A dark, almost dangerous smile curves his lips, and the muscles of my lower belly twist pleasurably. "I'm not going to suffocate, angel. I'll be too busy making you come."

He's bigger than me, and stronger. It's not really all that surprising he's able to overpower my objections. I squeak, my hands finding the top of the richly upholstered headboard as he pulls me into place. My hips are still hovering a few inches over his mouth, and Asher tilts forward, running his tongue through my slit with a low groan. "You taste so fucking good." He grips my ass in both hands and takes another lick, dragging the flat of his tongue over my throbbing clit.

I'm biting my lip so hard I'm going to draw blood, and the muscles in my abdomen ache with how hard I'm trying to keep it together. I feel so vulnerable like this, spread open with nowhere to hide, but it's hard to be self-conscious when the man with his face in my pussy so clearly loves it. "Oh god, daddy—"

I didn't even *mean* to call him that, but Asher groans his approval. "That's right, angel. Don't be shy."

His words make me tremble. Something heady and seductive is rising inside me, driving away any self-consciousness and guilt. It feels so good to surrender, to let him take charge and use my body as he sees fit. I don't have to think about anything; I just need to be a good girl and do what he says, and he'll make me feel good in return.

Moaning, I lower myself a little more, just enough for my soaked sex to skim over his lips. It's not close enough for Asher, though. Letting out an impatient growl, he drags me down, pushing my core *hard* onto his waiting mouth.

A part of me thought last week had been a fluke. Surely this man couldn't *actually* enjoy eating my pussy *this* much.

Ruby has talked to me about her sex life—in depth— and she has never once mentioned anything close to what happened last week. I get why he was holding back: He's a good person and wouldn't have wanted to sleep with me under false pretenses. That's been cleared up, though, and *still* he doesn't seem interested in anything other than melting my brain with as many orgasms as humanly possible.

It's working.

Overthinking about why has been officially suspended, and my fingers tighten painfully on the headboard as heat begins to coil low in my belly. I don't have to do or be anything right now, I just have to take what he gives me. I'm a different person, transformed by the touch of the man between my legs, and a piece of myself I didn't know was missing is slotting into place.

He's feasting on me, licking and sucking at every inch of my sex as his stubble rasps over my sensitive skin. Even the slow, wet sounds of his mouth working are impossibly sexy and intimate. It's so good—*he* is so good. Already, my legs are starting to shake, and as I begin to roll my hips, Asher's hands tighten on my ass to guide my pace. I'm his puppet, his horny little toy. And as he laps decadently at my throbbing clit, I can't remember why I was so worried about this.

I *like* that he's seeing me like this, in a way no one else ever has.

"Please, *please*." I hardly know what I'm saying, or if I'm saying anything at all, while gasping and moaning. All the muscles in my tummy have gone tense, and I'm strung tight, suspended over the edge but can't quite fall. My head tilts back, the ends of my hair brushing against my lower back as I grind down, mindless and desperate for more. Two of Asher's fingers dip into my wetness and move back, rubbing gentle circles over my *other* hole.

I fall apart, my entire body shaking as Asher licks me through it. A moment later, the world goes upside down. Somehow I'm on my back, and Asher is looming over me, chest heaving and eyes wild. The material of his boxers brushes against the sensitive skin of my inner thighs, and we both look down. His erection is straining against the thin layer of fabric separating us, only inches from my center. Slowly, he lowers his hips, sawing his ridged length through the lips of my pussy. I'm hypnotized by the sight, and my thighs part wider, instinctively offering him more.

"Such a horny little angel," Asher mutters, sounding almost angry as he shifts his weight onto one arm. A rough hand finds my breast, cupping and teasing roughly. "Can't believe how wet you get for me." He lifts his hips and I whine at the loss, but the sight of the front of his boxers drenched with my arousal makes it almost worth it.

"Please fuck me, daddy." I can't believe those words are actually coming out of my mouth, but I'm way past caring. *I need him.*

Need to feel his thick length filling the space inside me that is suddenly aching and empty.

Need to make him feel as good as he just made me.

Asher leans forward to nip at my bottom lip and

soothes the little sting with a gentle kiss. "I'm not sure you'd like that so much, angel. My cock is too big for you."

"I don't care." My legs spread wider, offering myself up to him. He's probably right, it would hurt, but that isn't the problem he seems to think it is. "I need to feel it."

He groans, and the smallest tremor runs through his body. "Not yet, angel. I'm not going to fuck you until you trust me, until you trust *this*."

My heart stalls.

"It's okay," Asher murmurs, sensing my silent panic. He lowers his head, leaving hot, open-mouthed kisses over my collar bone. "We're going to take our time. Do this right."

He said he wanted to keep seeing me, but we didn't get into specifics. Asher assuaged his guilt, he could fuck me with a clean conscience, but *do this right*? My heart flutters, despite the warning bells going off in my head.

"I do trust you," I blurt out, working to swallow the lump suddenly lodged in my throat. It's the truth. I'm not sure there's anyone I trust more.

It's myself I don't trust. Myself and my ability to be the kind of person who could deserve Asher Roth.

His hold on me tightens. "You don't. Not yet. You're holding back, and that's okay. Until today, you thought a lot of things about me, *about us*, that weren't true. It's going to take time. I'm going to show you I'm not fucking around."

The hand still cradling my breast moves up, pressing flat over the place where my heart pounds wildly beneath my rib cage. My head is spinning, and I can't keep up with the whiplash of emotions going on inside me. He's telling me everything I've ever wanted, fulfilling my wildest fantasies, but I'm not overjoyed.

Instead, I'm gripped by that same vulnerable, terrified

feeling that I was on my first day of college. He wants me now, or he thinks he does, but what will he say when he knows the truth? What will he say when he realizes I don't know the first thing about how to love someone when no one has ever loved me? Maybe it's wrong, maybe it makes me a coward and a liar, but if I tell him the truth, I might lose all of him; my friend, and my lover. Not to mention, possibly, my living arrangement.

It seems like keeping my heart out of this is impossible, but I can't be stupid.

I can't go all in. Not yet.

Asher lifts his head, and I meet his gaze, carefully composing my expression into something that *isn't* emotionally wrecked. "Sorry." He huffs a laugh, smiling crookedly. "I know I'm putting a lot on you tonight."

"You're not." I don't exactly sound convincing, though. All week I've been careful to manage my expectations, keeping Ruby's warnings in the back of my mind. I never expected that I'd walk in here and Asher would be ready to change the entire playing field. I'm scrambling to process the jumbled mess of my emotions in real time, and it's clearly not working. "Okay." I wince. "You might be. A little."

Asher's chuckle rumbles through his body and into mine. Pressed together like this, it's impossible to miss the ridge of his erection pressed snugly against my stomach. He's still hard—*really* hard—and I *really* want to touch it. "You're incredible." He grins, and warmth spreads through my belly as he lowers his lips to mine.

It's a deep, searching kiss, the kind that makes my whole chest feel like it's going to crack open, but not the kind that suggests he's trying to push things further than they've already gone. I *want* them to go further, though. I want him undone. This is a man who I *know* takes care of everyone else: his employees, his patients, and now me. He's so selfless, and in this moment, I hate it.

Taking advantage of his temporary distraction, I push my hand between our bodies and find the rigid length of his cock in seconds.

Above me, Asher stills, and I watch as his jaw tightens almost imperceptibly. I don't look away as I begin to stroke him up and down through the damp cotton, looking for signs he's about to shut this down and silence my protests with more earth-shattering orgasms. "Does that feel good?" I ask softly, heat pooling in my core when his hips jerk into my touch.

He lets out a low hiss between his teeth, his darkened gaze still fixed on my face. Emboldened, my hand moves beneath the waistband of his boxers. I love the way he feels in my hand, the softness of his skin and the steely hardness that pulses under my touch. Tightening my grip, I guide my thumb to the place just below the flared head and press, massaging gently.

Instantly, Asher shudders, his lips parting in surprise. *Victory.* "I'm not a little girl, daddy. Just because you haven't fucked me yet, doesn't mean I don't know some things." I murmur coyly as a fresh wave of wetness gathers at my entrance—a response to my own words. "You don't need to treat me like glass. I'm a lot harder to break than that."

"I don't—*fuckkkk.*" His hips jerk forward. "Adina, angel..."

I love it when he calls me that.

Biting my lip, I gaze up at him innocently. "Can I suck your cock? Please, daddy?" He watches, his chest heaving, as I swipe my thumb over the pre-cum beading at his slit and draw my hand up. When my lips close around the tip of my thumb, sucking it clean with a moan, I see his resolve break.

Asher allows me to push him over. He looks straight out of every fantasy I've ever had, sprawled on the bed with his hair a mess and bare chest heaving. I've wanted this for so long, to make this man feel just as good as he's made me feel.

He gives so much, but tonight, I want him to take.

"Are dentists usually this hot?" I muse, shifting so my legs are straddling one of his lean, muscular ones. Reaching out, I touch the line of dark-brown hair that trails from his belly button and disappears beneath the striped band of his boxers. Boxers that are stretched taut over his hardness.

Above me, there's a ragged laugh. "I'm thankful for the gym routine now that I need to keep up with a twenty-one-year-old."

Something tells me he wouldn't have a problem with that, even if he didn't work out. The man is insatiable.

"It's your own fault." I lower my head, gently kissing the tender patch of skin just above his waistband, and his cock twitches. As I brush the wet spot where pre-cum has soaked through the cotton, heat flairs low in my belly.

He helps me pull his boxers out of the way. Tempting as it may be to stare at him for ages, to draw this out, I know it's not going to happen the moment his cock is free. Pre-cum is dripping steadily into that trail of dark hair, and we both moan when I grasp the base of his shaft and lick it away.

My core pulses as I wrap my lips around his head, feeling Asher's hands tangle in my hair. Wordlessly, he guides me lower, showing me how he likes to be sucked. It's hard to breathe when I begin, but it doesn't take long to understand the rhythm of it.

It's not fast. He isn't fucking my mouth, or pushing himself further than I can comfortably take. I have the impression that he's savoring this, and a quick peek up confirms that those piercing blue eyes are glued to me, taking in every worshipful swirl of my tongue and stroke of my hand. He watches every move I make, big chest heaving, his expression rapt and hungry.

"Keep going—*fuck*—yes, angel. Suck me. Suck daddy's cock."

Oh god.

I'm high on this, on the effect I'm having on him and even though my jaw aches and my knees are beginning to throb, I could do this all night. Every quiet hiss of pleasure or raspy groan of *"angel"* makes my head spin and wetness spread over my thighs.

The room is so quiet that every wet, shameless slurp and muffled sigh I make seems even louder. I should be embarrassed, but it only makes the desperation inside me notch higher.

I want to worship him.

I want to make him feel better than anyone else ever has.

Suddenly inspired, I pull back and—careful to keep my eyes locked with his—lower my tongue to lick the underside of his cock from root to tip, a moan on my lips.

Asher's jaw tightens. "That's right, lick it. *Fuckkkk—*"

His words turn to a raw groan as I do it again, leaving open mouthed, reverent kisses as I go. Pre-cum beads at his tip, and I suck it away, loving the salty, earthy taste of him. As I adjust my position, though, my bare pussy brushes against his calf. It was just an accident, but it felt so good to have some relief, and I can't help doing it again.

"Goddamn." He hisses when I lift my hips again, embarrassment crawling up my throat. I keep my eyes down, focusing on swirling my tongue and stroking him the way he seems to like. A second later, though, Asher's leg bends slightly beneath me, pressing against my pussy. "Ride my leg, angel. It turns me on. Go on, don't be shy."

I grip his cock harder, conflict warring inside me. Even after everything we've done so far, grinding myself all over him because I'm turned on by sucking his dick seems like *a lot*. While my mind isn't so sure, my body has obviously made up its mind. The slightest shift of my body over his makes me whine as the texture of his leg hair rasps over my swollen clit.

A low curse from above me makes the knot in my belly tighten, and suddenly I can't help it anymore. Rational thought is officially way past my capabilities right now, especially when my hips begin to roll over him and we both realize how wet I've gotten.

Asher's hips lift slightly, trying to feed me more of himself, and I gag when the head of his cock hits the back of my throat. The noise only seems to make him go harder, and I can barely do more than keep my mouth open as wide as I can and take what he's giving me. "Fuck, you're so hot. Gonna come down your throat. Would you like that?"

I moan in response, my own orgasm approaching so fast it's almost alarming. I've never come so fast in my life, even with Asher's face between my legs, and it's a dark thrill to realize I *like* this. It's desperate and frantic and a little demeaning, but I'm pretty sure I've never been so turned on. As my body begins to shake with the force of the orgasm that's about to overtake me, the theory seems to be confirmed.

The hands tightening in my hair are my only warning. A

second later, Asher is dragging my head down, holding me still with trembling hands as salty cum pours down my throat. I choke, unable to swallow fast enough. Even with my eyes streaming, though, my hips don't stop their frantic, shaky thrusts over his bent leg. Just as Asher's hands relax, I follow him over the edge, bucking and whining with my mouth still full of his cum and softening cock.

It seems to take a full minute for my body to stop writhing over his. As soon as I fall to the side, panting, Asher is hovering over me.

"You're incredible," he murmurs in between kisses, apparently not giving a damn about the taste of his own cum on my lips.

I cling to him, trembling. "I didn't know..." My words fall away, but Asher nods like he knows exactly what I'm trying to say.

"Me either." He sounds winded. Pulling back to meet my eyes, he cradles my face in one big hand.

Something is happening to us, too big and intense to put into words. Everything about this situation is so messed up—*I* am so messed up—but right now, nothing has ever felt more right.

We stay that way for ages, talking quietly with our bodies entwined in the center of the big hotel bed. I learn that his mother's name is Martha and she bullies all the other ladies in her assisted living complex into joining her tennis club. He also has an older brother, who's an attorney in Boston. When the conversation switches to his career, he confesses that he knew he wanted to be a dentist when he was assigned to shadow a classmate's father for career day in the eighth grade. I tell him about school, and my internship, and even my questionable coworkers at the coffee shop.

He wants to know more, I can tell, but he doesn't push. Just like that, I lose another piece of my heart to Asher Roth.

It's not without a price, though, and that price is burning, horrible guilt.

Finally, when the sweat has dried on our skin and goosebumps begin to rise on my skin, Asher rolls to the edge of the bed and helps me up. He steals another long kiss before heading toward a door, which must lead to the bathroom. "Take a shower with me?" he asks over his shoulder, as if the opportunity to see this man naked, wet, and covered in soap would be something I am physically capable of rejecting.

I'm in a trance as I follow him into the bathroom.

This one is smaller, but no less luxurious than the bathroom in the suite from last time. The mirror has already fogged with steam from the beautiful marble shower as I shut the door behind me. My poker face must not be as good as it used to be, because Asher frowns. "Everything okay?"

"Yup!" I slip past him into shower. Despite this reassurance, Asher still looks troubled as he gets in behind me. His hands find mine, and I allow him to pull me close, holding each other beneath the cascade of warm water.

"Tell me what's the matter?"

His voice rumbles through the ear I have pressed to his chest. It's a question, not an order. He's so gentle with me, so patient. For god's sake, I've all but thrown myself at the man and he won't have sex with me because he wants me to feel safe first. He wants me to trust him, and this poor guy has no idea that I'm the one who shouldn't be trusted. I'm the liar here, not him.

My chest feels like it's going to cave in. "I'm worried that you're going to find out more about me and realize I'm not worth all the trouble. I'm... I might be fucked up, Asher. Like, *really* fucked up."

"Adina." Asher's firm voice pulls me back from the ledge of a full-on mental spiral. Cautiously, I blink up at him. The bulk of his body shields my face from the spray of water, and some of the tension bleeds from my body. "I'm trying not to scare the hell out of you, but you don't need to worry about me going anywhere. I'm in this. If you're fucked up, we'll fix you, angel."

Allison,

I'm getting a little worried. I haven't gotten a note from you in a while. Is everything okay with school? Please let me know if you need to scale back on hours. I'll make it work. Your education is more important. Now, turning our attentions to an equally important matter... On the one-to-ten scale, where am I sitting?

<u>Why was the dentist arrested by the FBI?</u>

<u>For supplying false identiteeth!</u>

I think I have a solid eight on my hands. I'm 99% sure.
-Doctor Roth

Hilarious Joke

Doctor Roth,

I have good news and bad news.
The good news is that I'm totally fine. Sorry I
haven't written in a while, things have been crazy.
The bad news is that your joke is a 1 out of 10. I'm
sorry to be the one to tell you, but if you tell it to a
patient, you're going to lose a lot of cool-dentist points.

-A

P.S. I regret to inform you that labeling your joke as
hilarious, does not necessarily make it hilarious.

The joke ⟶ 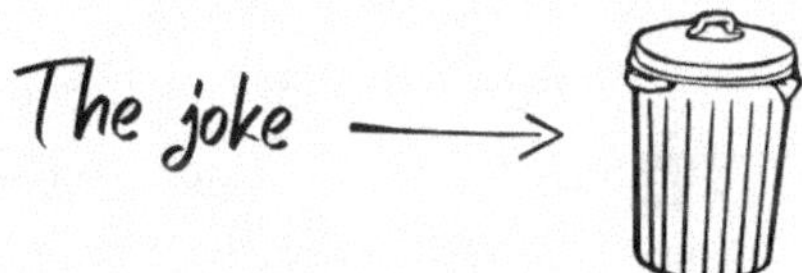

SHE STILL DOESN'T TRUST me.

It's been weeks, just over a month actually, since our second weekend at The Witt. We haven't been back. Instead, we spend weekends holed up in my minuscule apartment.

I'd been embarrassed to show her at first. The place had been hastily rented following my breakup, and I never bothered to decorate or do more than throw together a few flat-pack pieces of furniture. The night before she came for the first time, I went to a home decor store and frantically purchased plates, glasses, and silverware that wasn't plastic. It felt pathetic, being a grown man with his life together so poorly, but being able to serve my brand-new girlfriend dinner on plates that weren't left by the elderly woman who lived in my apartment before me was a start (the faded rose motif was a dead giveaway).

Adina wasn't disappointed in the apartment. If anything, she seems about a million times more comfortable and relaxed here than at The Witt, and I've even felt a growing fondness for the place since she started spending time here. Somehow, the ancient, heavily painted ceiling tiles and drafty windows feel less shabby and more quaint when Adina is kneeling on the floor in front of my coffee table, flashcards for her next test spread out before her.

She sleeps over sometimes during the week too, arriving past midnight with shadows beneath her eyes and smelling of stale coffee and the same kind of industrial cleaning supplies we have to use at the practice. Adina works harder than anyone I've ever met, flitting between school, an unpaid internship, and her two jobs in a caffeine-fueled blur. And, even with all that, she still makes time to make me feel like the luckiest man who's ever lived.

I'm in love with her.

There's no possible way around it, no way to dismiss the fierce, possessive feeling that grips me every time I look at her or think about her, or smell her shampoo on my pillow. In weeks, she's become the center of my whole world, and it's killing me to see her working her fingers to the bone, struggling, and not being able to do a thing about it.

Being open with her has, from the very first night we met, been easy for me. Even when I thought I wasn't capable of committing, even when I thought my lies would spell the end of us before we'd even begun, I couldn't help it. I can't count the number of times I've had to bite my tongue lately, stopping myself from asking more of her than she's ready to give.

It's a never-ending exercise in willpower to keep myself from telling her that I've fallen for her, that I'd marry her tomorrow if she let me, that *I'll take care of her.*

She wouldn't want that.

Adina is like a stray kitten I've been slowly winning over. She's starting to grow more comfortable with me, but one wrong move will erase all the progress we've made. All I can do is keep trying, keep being consistent, and *show* her exactly how much I adore her.

There are signs that it's working. Little things are beginning to shake loose from the wall she's built around her heart, tiny fragments of a dark early life. Her mother is dead and, like me, she never knew her father. Any of my casual, probing questions about who raised her or where she grew up have mostly been laughed off or rebuffed. She talks openly about her current life—her job at the coffee shop, her strange relationship with Ruby, her internship, and school—but anything before that is firmly off limits.

I have suspicions, and the desperate hope that I'm wrong about them, but that's all. Like it or not, I have to be patient with her and trust that the incredible woman I've fallen for will one day trust me enough to tell me everything. Sometimes, though, the self-doubt creeps in. Am I making a fool of myself, being so utterly committed to a woman I barely know? Especially one who happens to be half my age and so deeply guarded.

Those thoughts tend to come when we're apart, when I have time to *think* instead of *feel*.

As I open the door for her late on Friday night, though, just the sight of her is enough to ease all anxiety about our situation.

Adina sags with relief and shuffles forward, dropping her battered backpack on the floor in my little entryway. She wraps herself around me without hesitation.

Fuck. This woman.

"I missed you," she mumbles into my chest, and I press my lips to the top of her head. Even beneath the scent of coffee and cleaning supplies, I catch a hint of her sweet, floral scent. Just holding her is overwhelming.

How the hell am I supposed to play it cool? How the hell do I pretend I'm breathing properly for the first time since she last walked out the door? Drawing my hand up her spine, I pull her close, my heart in my throat. "I missed you too. Are you hungry?"

Adina nods, but makes no move to release me. We stand there, holding each other and not saying a word. I've never felt this kind of intimacy before, the comfort and familiarity of being held by the person you love with no need to speak, and I've become addicted. I want it every fucking day.

"Where are you going to live this summer? After you graduate?"

The words are out of my mouth before I can think better of it, and I regret it instantly as Adina's body tenses against mine.

Drawing back to peer up at me, her expression is guarded. "Why?"

I drag my thumb over her bottom lip, not allowing myself to show how her words have punctured the full, warm feeling that filled me so recently. Two steps forward, one step back. "Just wondering."

She looks worried. "Asher—"

"Come on, let me feed you." I draw away but keep my hand pressed to the base of her spine, guiding her into the little kitchen area. It's narrow, with graying white cabinets trimmed in fake vinyl wood. A lone two-person table is crammed into the corner with my laptop open on top of it beside a pile of tax documents. Adina takes the seat across from it, watching silently as I take the bag of Chinese takeout out of the fridge. "You can shut that." I indicate the computer with a grimace.

The beginning of the year always brings with it a visit to my accountant and the not-so-pleasant reminder of how close the practice has come to sliding from barely profitable to completely unsustainable. This year was better than most, but even so. Even with Adina in my life now, I feel myself edging closer to complete burnout and have no idea what to do about it. It's been years since I've taken a vacation, but I can't justify it or afford closing down the entire practice for any length of time.

"Looks like fun," Adina remarks dryly, tucking the documents back into their folder and closing the screen as I put the first container of food in the microwave.

I sigh, rubbing absently at the stubble on my jaw that has grown in since this morning. "Yes. We really need to hire another hygienist, but I can't imagine where we'll find room in the budget."

Her head tilts slightly. "Have you ever thought about becoming a nonprofit? It would be a long process, but there are a lot of benefits. For one, you could have other practices in the area send their staff over to help out, companies could donate equipment and supplies, and other dentists could offer their time. You'd be able to help so many more patients. The tax stuff too..." She trails off, looking thoughtful. "I'm not an expert or anything, but I took a few classes in nonprofit management last year and I could point you in the right direction."

"That's..." I trail off, my throat working as I gaze at her in complete disbelief. "Wow, angel. That's such an incredible idea. I never considered it."

"It was just a thought." She's adorable, trying to pretend she isn't too pleased with herself and my praise. The way she catches her bottom lip between her teeth to keep herself from smiling is a dead giveaway, though.

I push off the counter and cross to her. "You're incredible." She tilts her chin up, meeting my kiss with such obvious enthusiasm that my body responds instantly. Heat builds inside me, filling me just from the soft sound of her blissful sigh and the feeling of her hands on my shoulders. Behind me, the microwave beeps loudly. I straighten up reluctantly, giving her a look that plainly says what I plan to do to her once we're done eating.

Judging by her thighs subtly pressing together beneath the table, I'd consider the message received.

"I'm going to speak to my accountant and the practice's attorney next week to see if it's even an option," I tell her, excited now. It really is an excellent solution. Liam could probably be persuaded to throw a fundraiser at The Witt and have his many filthy-rich associates donate. I could get a *normal* job with *normal* hours, and donate my time instead of being chained to the damn building.

Allison is a worry, though. I doubt that a nonprofit manager would approve of me paying a cleaner in cash and letting her sleep on the couch in my office. Then again, she, like my girlfriend, will be graduating from college soon. The process of transitioning to a nonprofit could take years, and I'm positive she'll have moved on by then. It's the natural order of things, even if I'll be sorry to lose her. I want her to do better, to overcome whatever put her on that street three years ago.

Tonight, I'm not worrying about any of it, though. The relaxed, joyful feeling that Adina so often brings out in me is beginning to expand inside me, erasing the tension of the day. Things might not be perfect and we may still have a way to go, but *I'm happy* damn it. The woman of my dreams is sitting at my kitchen table right now, weighed down by her own worries. Tonight, we're going to set all that shit aside.

I want to play.

"I was thinking," I muse, careful to avoid looking at her directly as I busy myself with another take-out container. "We haven't been on a proper date yet."

A startled laugh sounds from behind me. "This is a date!"

The three-hour-old takeout sitting in front of me says otherwise. "*This* is me taking care of my girlfriend after she had a long day." I lean my hip against the counter and cross my arms. "I'm talking about *romance*, Adina Collier. Haven't you watched *Bridgerton*?"

"No, but I'm guessing you have." She's trying not to laugh, though, and I feel about ten feet tall. Making this woman smile has rapidly become the best part of my days. Admittedly, though, making her come on my face is a close second.

It's a monumental effort to stop my face from splitting in a huge grin. "So you *don't* want to go on a date then? Just to be clear."

My words are met with an exasperated huff from the beautiful creature before me. "I didn't say that."

With a thoughtful hum, I turn to take the last container out of the microwave. Adina is busying herself by gathering up the electronics and paperwork when I come up behind her with the plates, taking care to brush my chest against her back.

In the narrow kitchen, it would be easy enough to pass such a thing off as a side effect of the limited space, but we both know better.

Again and again as we set the table in companionable silence, I take care to touch her whenever possible. It's beyond satisfying to listen to the little hitch in her breathing as I rest my hand on the small of her waist for a few seconds, or see a pale flush beginning to crawl up her neck when I "accidentally" press her hips into the table with mine.

Keeping myself from fucking her has been almost as difficult as keeping my feelings in check. When she comes here at night, I'm somewhat prepared for it. It's the mornings that have truly tempted me to within an inch of my sanity. Having her in my bed, surrounded by the warm scent of honey and wildflowers, seeing her tousled hair and bare face while feeling her perfect, perky ass press against my cock... Half asleep, the urge to drive my length inside her wet heat is instinctual. There's no way to prepare for it, no way to ward it off, and every time it brings me closer to a ledge I don't dare acknowledge.

"Did you get the forks?" My hand splays flat on her lower belly, and I pretend it's merely so I can kiss her cheek gently.

She isn't fooled. "You're teasing."

"Am I?"

"*Yes.*"

"*Hmm,*" I hum, brushing my lips over the slope of her neck. Pressing her body against mine more firmly, I know there's no way for her to miss the throbbing length of my erection pressed against her lower back.

The food lays inches away from us, but we've already forgotten about it. The world has narrowed down to just us two. Nothing else matters.

"Asher," she breathes, grinding back against me.

"Do you need me, angel?" My hands move to the place on her waist where they fit so perfectly.

Shakily, she nods. "Yes."

I nip at her pale, perfect earlobe. From my vantage point, I watch as the tip of her tongue darts out, wetting her lips. "You know how to ask."

"Please?"

"I think you can do better than that." My hands tighten on her waist.

Adina's entire body quakes, her eyelids fluttering shut. "Will you make me come? Please, daddy?"

She never sees it coming.

One moment, my horny little thing is rubbing her ass against my hard cock, and the next she's doubled over in fits of laughter.

"Can't believe you thought *this* was a date." I laugh, my hands dancing over her sides, mercilessly tickling her.

Squealing, Adina tries to make a break for it and we both nearly fall through the living room doorway, a chair clattering noisily to the floor in our wake.

"I'm sorry! I'm sorry!" She's laughing so hard there are tears in her eyes, and still I don't stop, wrestling with her all the way to the couch.

She's so much smaller than me that it would be nearly effortless to overpower her, but I let her get the upper hand for a moment, my own laughs joining hers as we tumble onto the cushions in a tangled mess of limbs.

"And you'll let me take you out tomorrow night?" I gather her wrists in one hand and pin them above her head, grinning down into her shining face. I've never heard her laugh like this, completely unrestrained and free.

Adina laughs harder, wriggling helplessly beneath me as her breath comes in big, gasping gulps in between peels of laughter. "Yes!" she manages to squeal, and, triumphant, I decide to give her a whole new reason to lose her breath.

fourteen

ADINA

NOT MANY PEOPLE feel safe at the dentist's office.

I get it. Best case scenario, you have gloved fingers poking around in your mouth while you're peppered with questions about how often you floss or whether you've thought about buying one of those fancy supersonic toothbrushes that eviscerate plaque. Worst case, there's something wrong and you need to have someone drill a hole in one of your teeth while you drool all over yourself.

Granted, dental care in the foster care system isn't exactly top-notch, and god knows I don't have insurance now, but I don't live under a rock. Objectively, the whole process kind of sucks, and I'm guessing it says a lot about me that Asher Roth's practice is my happy place. For three years, it's been my refuge, my one point of stability that I could absolutely count on. I didn't have a lease or even a bed, but I trusted the kind doctor in the ridiculous lab coats.

I told myself not to do it. I remembered all the times I thought I was safe and secure but wasn't, but still it

151

happened. Somewhere along the way, I allowed myself to put down the shallowest, tiniest of roots.

Roots that might be ripped up any day now, because I can't keep lying to him. *I can't.*

Will Asher think I took advantage of him? Will he believe me when I tell him that meeting in that hotel was the wildest, strangest coincidence of all time, or will he think I targeted him somehow? My heart, which has belonged to Asher Roth for years now, trusts him unconditionally. My brain is equally as confident that he's going to think I'm a crazy stalker and throw me out on my butt.

My only hope is to tell him the rest of the story too. To shine a light into all the dark corners of my life I've worked so hard to keep buried.

It hasn't worked, though. Not really. The situation I'm in now is a direct result of where I came from and my bid to escape it. I'm proud of how far I've come—really I am—but now I want more. I want *him*, and I'm so sick and tired of holding back.

My happy place, the place I feel safest, isn't in Doctor Roth's office anymore. It's right here, curled beneath the covers in his little apartment with the warmth of his naked body seeping into mine as morning light filters in through the blinds. I've been up for hours, staring blankly at the cracked plaster of the wall across from me, turning everything over in my head.

In moments like this, I feel a million miles removed from the night we met. I'm not cold or numb or lost anymore, because this man had my back. Not once, not twice, but every single day for the last three years. He deserves the truth, even if it shatters me to tell it.

I've always told myself that I am brave when I need to be... Well, I need to be now. Last night was the closest I've ever come to being happy, and the only thing more painful than the thought of losing everything is holding myself back from feeling like that every day.

How long have I been living in this half-alive state, standing in the shade when the sun is steps away? Ages.

After hours of thinking, of turning the situation over in my mind as Asher holds me, I keep coming to the same conclusion. By the time he stirs, mumbling words I can't hear as he gathers me close, something has slotted into place in my chest—a grim sort of acceptance.

"Shouldn't you be at the coffee shop?" he murmurs, voice raspy with sleep.

I shake my head, still staring at the spider web of cracks in his plaster wall. Someone tried to cover the whole mess up with a thick layer of paint, but it's only a matter of time before it all comes crumbling down.

Yeah, I won't treat my relationship with this incredible person the same way his shitty landlord treated these walls.

"I texted my boss and said I had food poisoning." My fingers drift over the hair scattering the back of his arm, my throat tight. I've never called in before. Ever. The loss of income sucks, but today I just couldn't stomach dragging myself across town to serve shitty burnt coffee and crappy donuts while this brand-new resolution hangs over my head.

Asher's chest shakes in a silent laugh as he pulls me closer, pressing a bristly kiss to my bare shoulder. "I get you all to myself? For a full day?"

God, he sounds so happy. It's tempting to roll my hips back, to grind my ass against his morning wood and lose myself in the chemistry that's always come so easily for us. Maybe we'd spend all day in bed, touching each other. Maybe we wouldn't have to say a single word.

Instead, I exhale shakily, my eyes still glued to that cracked plaster. "Can we talk?"

Asher stills. "Is everything okay?" There's trepidation in his voice—fear—like he's afraid I'm about to break up with him or something. As if it never occurred to him that *he* might want to end this. Maybe it hasn't.

"There are things I haven't told you. About… me." Granted, I don't have much experience (*any* experience) in telling people my story, but there aren't exactly a ton of ways to sugar coat it or ease into it. Even thinking about where to start sends coldness through me. Closing my suddenly burning eyes, I focus on the parts of my body where my skin is pressed against Asher's, allowing it ground me.

He doesn't say a word, but his hold on me tightens, like he knows I need it without me having to ask.

"I was born about an hour upstate. My mom was a drug addict. If my father was involved at any point, I don't remember him. She bounced between men a lot. Most of them were dealers or other users, and none of them were kind." I pause, refocusing on Asher's warmth and not the countless horrible memories threatening to bubble to the surface.

I'm here now. I'm safe.

"There was a lot of moving around. Sometimes I went to school, sometimes I didn't. Sometimes my mom was interested in me, but mostly she wasn't. I definitely remember social workers getting involved a few times. She must have cared a little, because she always made sure I was clean and the apartment was okay before the people with clipboards showed up." I close my eyes, remembering the probing questions from the professionally dressed strangers that I was too afraid to answer. "Even then, I knew life wasn't supposed to be so hard, but it was all I knew."

Behind me, Asher's body has gone tense, and I can tell he's trying to keep his breathing even without much success. For some reason, the knowledge that my pain is having this kind of effect on him makes me feel even worse, and it's all I can do to not break down.

There are plenty of terrible parts, but the worst part of this story that I was dreading most is here. "The drug use got worse when I was about eight. When I was ten she overdosed. I... found her one morning. The guy we were staying with had booked it, and the house was so cold I just thought she was sleeping."

I feel the burn of the cold even now. It's so real that a tremor runs through my body, like I'm there again and not safe in bed with a man who adores me. Asher presses his lips to my shoulder, and I swear I feel his muscles quake too. "I'm so sorry," he whispers against my skin, his voice breaking.

Have I ever connected with anyone enough for my grief to become theirs as well?

We lay in silence for a long time while Asher holds me so tightly it's almost painful, but I don't want him to loosen his arms.

I'm here now.

I'm safe.

I'm safe.

I'm safe.

He doesn't ask me to speak or ask any questions. It takes a long time to free myself from that horrible, icy morning, but finally I do.

I realize that I can keep going, and when I begin to speak, my voice is stronger than before. "It was foster care after that. None of my foster parents were bad people, I was the problem... I was so *angry*." I shake my head miserably, filled with shame for how I'd once treated perfectly nice, kind people who opened their home to me. "I think I wanted to be in control, for once. I pushed them away. I broke rules and acted out. I was a little asshole. It seemed like it was easier, you know? To decide you wanted to go instead of waiting to be sent away. I smoked, I drank, and I ruined things for the sake of it. My life was out of control."

"I would have been angry too." Asher's head shakes slightly, his voice a low, strained prayer in my ear. "None of this is your fault, Adina."

The gaping, hollow wound in the center of my chest, the one I try my best to ignore, is raw now.

"Maybe," I concede, lifting my shoulder in a feeble attempt at indifference. "By the time I turned sixteen, I'd been in over a dozen foster homes. There aren't many families willing to take in kids like that, so I landed in a group home in Albany. There were about thirty girls living there, and most of us were troubled, bad kids. The ones no one wanted. Really early on, I got on the wrong side of this group of girls. They absolutely ran the place and they started going after me pretty badly. The staff wasn't being paid enough to care."

Asher curses quietly, tensing as though he's ready to protect me.

I smile tightly. "Yeah. Our tax dollars at work, right?"

"Don't." There's a harsh edge of anger to the word. "Don't minimize this, Adina."

We're getting close to the point of no return, to the biggest, hardest truth of all of this. I push forward. "Either I took their shit and got beat on, or I told someone and got beat on harder for being a snitch. I couldn't win, you know?

I ran away, but I didn't make it long on my own. Only a few weeks after I left, it started getting cold. I went to a shelter, but they realized I was a runaway and called the police, who then brought me straight back to the group home."

I'd laid on my side, sobbing into the back seat of the police cruiser and begging them not to bring me back. I couldn't bear to go back to that place, where every single person hated me. Nobody wanted to get on the bad side of those girls, and they'd rather trip me on the stairs than be tripped themselves. I was their designated punching bag, and nobody wanted to nominate themselves as my replacement.

I understood, but that didn't make it any easier.

"When I was seventeen, I kind of lost it. In retrospect, I think I must have been really depressed..."

That last day at the group home, when those girls pulled me into a supply closet to cut off my hair and beat me for taking the last orange juice carton at breakfast, something in me snapped. I didn't care where I went or what happened to me, but I couldn't take it anymore.

"I ran away again, only this time I did it a little better. I had enough money to get on a train to the city. There was some shitty telemarketer job I thought I could get with my fake ID. That didn't work out, and neither did any of my other half-baked ideas. That was it for me. I couldn't go back, but I was also terrified of asking for help. I really thought nobody cared."

I open my mouth, then close it again. This is it, the part where he comes in, because I was wrong about nobody caring. Asher cared. He didn't even know me, but he saw me. Something made him stop, something made him risk letting a homeless runaway into his practice unattended. A part of me was hoping I would get to this part and he would realize on his own. That, maybe, he'd pick up on all the little fragments of me he's gathered from my time as his girlfriend and as Allison, and *know*.

Then, slowly—*miraculously*—Asher's arm curls further around me, and he's pulling me over to face him.

My heart is lodged in my throat, and the fear and hope swelling inside me have grown so big that they take up all the room in my chest. I can barely breathe. When I can finally see his face, there is no anger or shock. He's sad for me, grief-stricken, but he hasn't realized why I've stopped talking.

"Asher—" A desperate sob escapes my throat. I try to speak, but nothing comes out.

His hand cradles my face, and he leans forward to kiss me gently, with such tenderness it makes my battered heart ache. When he pulls away, he doesn't go far. "I love you." He says the words like he's never meant anything more, low and desperate and deathly serious. "I'm in love with you, angel. You'll never have to be alone again. Not if you don't want to be."

Oh god.

Never have I wanted anything more than to hear someone say those words to me. I've been alone for so long, walking through this city like a ghost, because I was too scared of getting hurt again to try and connect with anyone. Maybe I didn't know how.

The resolution I was so recently filled with has gone cold. Asher doesn't know everything, not yet, but he *loves* me. He knows where I come from now, knows enough to understand, right? I'll tell him. I will. I'll tell him, and it's going to be okay. Not now, though, because in this moment there's only one possible thing I can say.

"I love you too."

Triumph flares in those bright-blue eyes, and then he's kissing me again, pressing me back into the pillows with an intensity that steals the breath from my lungs. It's raw and messy and frantic. We're claiming each other, and never in my life have I been so sure that something was right.

Maybe—just *maybe*—I was meant for this man, and he was meant for me.

Maybe the whole universe has been conspiring, subtly putting things in order so we'd find each other, and now that we have...

Maybe things will turn out okay.

Maybe.

Despite what I just told him and the things I still need to say, I've never felt freer than I do right now. Hope is blooming inside me, and when Asher draws back, panting, to press his forehead against mine, in seconds I've pulled him back in.

"Please," I whisper against his lips, and the muscles low in my belly knot when his cock—already hot and hard— twitches against my hip.

He groans quietly as I smooth my hands up his arms, trying to erase the sudden tension I feel there. He's strung tight, holding himself back. "We don't have to do this now." His voice is like gravel.

I get why he's apprehensive. After all, I was crying all over him a few minutes ago. I told him things I've never told anyone, things I've barely dared to think about myself. "I'm okay. I swear." My hands find his face, and I force him to meet my eyes as my pulse throbs unevenly. "I'm just... I'm so sick of holding back."

His eyes search mine, searching for signs of apprehension or lingering pain, but I know he won't find any.

I see the moment his resolve breaks. One moment we're

staring at each other, and then, with a low groan, Asher Roth is kissing me. It's just like before, like we didn't stop at all. Desperation and heat are building between us, and my head spins as he drags his body over mine. My thighs fall open to make space for him, and we both groan as the head of his cock bumps against my swollen clit.

We haven't been this close since our first night together at The Witt, and I always got the sense that Asher didn't want to test himself. Like if his cock was nestled between the lips of my pussy with my wetness coating his thick shaft, the temptation to draw back just a little and push inside would be too much to resist.

"Fuck, angel." Asher groans as I buck against him, trying in vain to get him where I need him most. I've never felt so empty, and the muscles of my core clench greedily with every roll of my hips, desperate to be stretched around him. *Finally.*

Lowering his head, he sucks one of my pebbled nipples between his lips, grazing the sensitive flesh with his teeth. I writhe beneath him, arching my back and spreading my thighs as wide as I can. It feels so good to have his whole weight on top of me, pressing me down into the mattress. He's so much bigger than me; I feel small and defenseless and claimed.

Why does that turn me on so much—the thought of this bigger, older, and more experienced man using my body however he wants? Taking his pleasure in the place I've saved just for him. "Fuck me," I plead, almost shaking with need. "However you want, just please—" My words turn to a gasp when a big hand shoves between our bodies and suddenly, two fingers are circling my entrance.

Releasing my breast, Asher stares down at me, his jaw tight. My lips part, and I make a noise somewhere between a cry and a whine as he pushes them inside me, filling me in a single stroke. "Do you feel that?" he grits out, and I squeak as those thick fingers spread out inside me, stretching my walls until they burn. "Does it hurt?"

I nod shakily, but he adds a third finger and my lips parting in a silent moan.

Asher's gaze darkens. "My dick is bigger than that. Are you going to let me get you ready, or are you an impatient little thing who wants it now?"

God. I love dirty-talking Asher.

I'm not sure what I expected. After all, we've done everything *but* have sex at this point, and I'm very familiar with his growly, possessive side. This is a man who only last week bent me over the kitchen table, pulled down my panties, and spanked me raw for daring to ask whether he'd like me to pay for half of dinner.

Despite all the waiting and buildup, I think I imagined slow, devoted lovemaking for our first time.

I probably should have known better.

My tongue darts out to wet my lips, the tiniest sliver of apprehension now joining the burning excitement. "I'm impatient, daddy. I want it right now."

Asher's groans. "Put your legs around my waist. Yeah, like that. Good girl."

Holy crap. We're doing this. *Finally.*

His eyes flash as I reach down to wrap my hand around the base of his shaft. He allows me to guide the head of his cock to my entrance, pulling his fingers free so I have room to fit us together.

The apartment is quiet. All I can hear is our ragged breathing and the soft rustle of bedding as he nudges forward, not quite entering me but threatening to. The slightest flex of his hips, and we'd be joined.

"Try to relax, alright? Hold on to me."

I nod breathlessly, my heart hammering against my rib cage as my hands settle on his broad shoulders. For a moment, it's like we're suspended in time, gazing at each other in silent acknowledgment of what's coming.

Then, Asher's lips find mine, and my sharp cry is muffled by his kiss as he pushes forward, opening me.

"Shhh." He pauses as I adjust to the overwhelming sensation of my body being filled by his, dropping hot, lingering kisses over the delicate skin below my jaw. Nothing can distract me from the intense pressure between my legs, though.

Holy crap. He's *inside* me right now.

I shift restlessly, instinctively trying to find more room for him, but it isn't possible.

Asher's hand tightens in my hair, and he pushes a little deeper before stopping again, pulsing slightly in and out. "Such a good girl." He groans. "God angel, you have no idea how good you feel."

The stretch is so much—*too much*—but his praise has ignited a new heat inside me. I've never belonged to someone before, but now I do. Asher is making me his, and even if it always hurts this much, I'll still beg for him to do this to me every single day.

It won't hurt this much again, though. I know that. Already, tension I didn't realize I had is beginning to bleed from my internal muscles, and somehow the pressure of his cock pressing against my walls is soothing the same ache it created.

Tentatively, I rock my hips slightly, and he slides a little further. My back bows off the bed, a gasp catching in my throat.

Asher groans. "That's it—*that's fucking it.* Going to give you the rest now, okay?"

My answering laugh is shaky and breathless. "I don't think there's room."

I'm joking. Mostly. Admittedly, as I look down and see how tightly I'm stretched around him and how much more of his thick shaft there's still to take, I may have some concerns about the logistics of this.

Taking my face in his hand, Asher drags my chin back up, forcing my gaze back onto him. "I'll make room."

ASHER

I'M TOO FAR GONE to slow this down.

The sight of her spread open for me, her gorgeous little pussy clutching greedily at my cock... *Fuck*. I'm going to remember fucking Adina Collier's virginity away for the rest of my life, and I'll be damned if that memory doesn't include her face when she realizes she's taken all of me.

This is happening, and I'll make sure she loves it. I need her addicted to me, need her to want this as badly as I do, because I will never get enough of her. My strong, resilient miracle girl, who was thrown in my path to make me realize everything I've been missing. She was made for me, and now I'll prove it to her.

My dark proclamation has barely left my lips before I'm driving forward again, pushing my length the rest of the way into her hot channel before she has time to tense up. It's a tight fit, even with how wet she is, but her body opens for me anyway. I want to throw my head back, to close my eyes and bask in the white-hot pleasure coursing up my spine, but I stare down at her face instead.

It's worth it.

My girl's expression is part shock, part innocent wonder as she stares to the place we're connected.

"You did it, angel," I murmur, biting back the urge to do more than rock gently in and out, easing things. "How does it feel?"

Adina whimpers, her wide eyes darting up to meet mine. "Like you're touching me everywhere."

Christ—I love that.

A groan rumbles in my chest as I pull back a few inches and thrust back into her, giving her that first true taste of what it's going to be like to be fucked. Beneath me, angel gasps, digging her fingers into my shoulders like she's not sure if she wants to push me away or pull me closer.

It's a lot, I get it. I should be going slower, should be easing us *both* into this—because I sure as hell haven't felt anything like this either—but as another wave of slick eases my way... *Fuck.* It's all I can do to keep myself from pinning her to the mattress and using her tight, wet cunt until neither of us can tell where my body ends and hers begins.

Nothing has ever felt so good. She's tighter than I knew was possible, and while I should be sorry I'm putting her through this, the knowledge that I'm the only man to ever be inside her is enough to shatter whatever sane, rational parts are left of me. She's mine—*only* mine—and I won't be letting her go. Ever.

I hadn't realized how badly I needed this connection with her, and as I find a deep, grinding rhythm, I could tip my head back and howl. How many times have I leaned against the shower wall, working my cock and wishing I could find relief between her thighs instead? Too many to count. I've imagined this in every conceivable position— imagined her sweet and shy, desperate and wanton, confident and hungry—yet no fantasy has ever come close to how exquisite this really feels.

"God." Adina gasps, her breaths coming in sharp pants as her inner walls begin to flutter over my cock.

The rough, animalistic growl I make in response is nothing short of feral. She's ready for more. Pulling back until only the head of my cock is inside her, I drive back down, and her cry of shock is joined by the wet, sloppy sounds of our bodies working together.

"Not god," I hiss as I withdraw again. "Daddy." I'd thought it was fucked up once, her calling me that in bed, but I see clearly now how utterly perfect it is. I want to be her *everything*, her provider and caretaker, her lover and friend. I want to be the man who pounds her virgin pussy into my mattress and makes her breakfast in bed afterward. The sound of any other name—man, biblical being, or otherwise —on her lips when my cock is inside her, makes me furious.

"Daddy!" Adina amends breathlessly, pulling me down for a short, hot kiss, as my thrusts drive her further up the bed. Beneath us, the mattress creaks in time with my pace, and I had no idea a shitty old spring could be so erotic.

I hope my asshole neighbor, the guy who leers at Adina when we walk past him in the lobby, can hear us through the wall. The thought makes me grit my teeth, and I reach down to hitch her leg higher on my hip. "Let me hear you," I plead, bearing down on her, and the headboard hits the wall noisily with each thrust. "Scream for me, angel."

She comes with a loud cry, her pussy clamping down on my dick, and I have to bite the inside of my cheek to keep from following.

We've barely begun. The way I feel right now... once isn't going to be enough for tonight. Not even close. I'm a horny, middle-aged man who is balls-deep in a gorgeous college girl, and I'm going to make it *last*, damn it. I'm addicted. She's going to find herself in this position as often as she'll let me, pumped full of my cum morning, noon, and night. Even that might not sate the monster this woman has created of me.

This time, though, our first time... Well, I'm going to draw it out. Going to give her something to remember.

She's barely collapsed back onto the mattress, her eyes hazy in the aftermath of her orgasm, before I'm dragging myself free. She gazes up at me, panting, as my hands find her hips. "Ass in the air, beautiful."

She obeys instantly, scrambling over onto her knees and lifting that round little ass in offering. It's the work of seconds to fist the base of my shaft—still sticky from her cum—and guide myself back to her opening.

The sight of my thick shaft pressing into her eager little hole is hypnotizing. I can get closer this way, and we both hiss as I hit bottom, the tip of my cock pressed snugly against the deepest part of her.

My hands ghost over her beautiful curves. "I'm not wearing a condom. Can I come inside you?"

Beneath me, Adina wriggles, her legs spreading wider as she instinctively tries to make extra room for my erection. "I have an IUD," she whispers raggedly, and I reward her with a short, sharp thrust that makes her squeak in surprise. "Will you—" Her words falter, and a pink flush begins to crawl up her neck.

Christ, she's so fucking eager. "You want me to come inside you?" I guess, my hips beginning to pulse in long, steady thrusts that make both of us groan.

She nods against the pillow, her eyes fluttering shut as

her sweet pussy clutches greedily at my cock. "Yes please, daddy."

No fucking problem.

"Touch your clit," I growl, moving faster now, and the room is filled with the crude, wet noise of slapping skin all over again.

Adina obeys immediately, her lips parting in a long moan when that hand slips between her spread thighs. "Daddy, it feels good."

Holy shit, I'm going to come so hard. There's no holding it back, not anymore, but she needs to get there first. Every muscle in my body is strung tight to keep myself from blowing too soon and, desperately, my hand comes down on her ass in a sharp slap.

Apparently, that's all my girl needs to send her over the edge.

Adina finishes with a loud sob, her cunt clamping down, and I couldn't pull out even if I wanted to. She's got me locked down, and all I can do is fall forward over her as my orgasm crashes over me like a wave.

I doubt I've ever come so much. It goes on forever, long spurts of cum pouring out of me and filling her. This is incredible—*she* is incredible—and I'm fucking addicted. Even when the last of the pleasure fades away and my cock is softening, I still don't pull out.

Instead, I fall to the side, curling myself around her back and showering reverent kisses over the damp skin of her shoulder. "*Fuck.*" I groan, loving the intimacy of being connected to her, and also the idea of my cock keeping all that cum inside her.

Adina hums, arching her back so her ass is resting snugly in my lap, sealing us together. "That was amazing. I'm officially a big fan of sex."

I chuckle, my hand finding the soft warmth of her breast and cradling it against my palm. "It's not like that every time, angel. Don't get any ideas."

For fuck's sake, I'm the one who mentioned it, yet hot licks of jealousy are still rising inside me.

"No worries." She reaches back over her shoulder to play with my hair. "I have a thing for cute, glasses-wearing dentists who are sweet to me every hour of the day, except when we're naked."

"That's very specific."

Adina hums in happy agreement. "Are you complaining?"

Hah.

"How do you feel?" My hand moves from her breast down to her lower belly, pressing into the soft skin beneath her bellybutton. Adina sighs happily, squirming in my lap.

"Sore." Instantly, I move to draw back, but her hand clamps down on my arm, stopping me. "No, don't. I like having you inside me."

I swallow as heat begins to settle at the base of my spine again. "I'm going to get hard again. If you're too sore…"

She still doesn't release my arm, but we both relax, settling back into the mattress as the old radiator beneath the window clanks noisily to life. Outside, fluffy snowflakes are settling on the windowsill. Despite the intensity of everything she told me and the frantic hunger of the sex we just had, I've never felt more at peace.

The things I learned about her past are horrible, yet the fact she overcame it makes me even more in love with her. She's incredible, and now I know she wants the same things that I do. We have time, all the time in the world, and I don't have to hide how I feel about her anymore.

Adina doesn't know it yet, but I've just made it my life's mission to make sure she never feels alone or unloved ever again.

"You know," I muse, reaching behind me to pull a blanket over us both. "I don't think we ever settled the results of the favorite food search."

Adina sighs wistfully, turning her head to kiss the arm I have slipped under her. "I *loved* those tacos."

"Those were the first thing you tried! You can't pick the first thing, Adina," I object playfully, my fingers dancing threateningly over her side. She giggles, squirming a little, and my cock throbs. The slight movement is enough to make heat prickle through my abdomen.

Goddamn, that was fast.

"I picked you on the first try," she reminds me coyly.

Damn right, she did.

My hand slips down to press against her lower belly, holding her firmly in place. I want her to feel exactly what she does to me.

"You have the most beautiful body, angel," I murmur, ghosting my lips over her bare shoulder. "These curves..."

Adina sucks in a ragged breath, and I know she's feeling it as blood rushes to my dick and I begin to harden again inside her. "Holy crap," she whispers, the muscles in her belly spasming beneath my hand.

I don't hurry this along, just lay still, murmuring quiet praise into her ear as my cock swells. I've never done this before, but it's exquisite. "Does it hurt?" I ask when I'm fully seated, pushing my hand between her thighs to rub gentle circles over her swollen clit.

She trembles, arching closer. "Yes, but in a good way."

Without another word, I roll over, pressing her into the mattress. As I begin to move and Adina lets out her first ragged moan, a sharp banging on the wall makes us both pause, looking up.

"For christ's sake!" comes the muffled yell of my leering neighbor. "I get it!"

Yeah, I'm sure he does. Just to be sure, though, I lift Adina into my arms and cross the small room to fuck her against the wall.

Doctor Roth,
I'm so sorry to do this to you, but would it be possible to have tomorrow night off? Something important came up, and I really want to do it. If it's inconvenient in any way, please let me know and I'll take care of the cleaning after the event. It just might be a while later than usual.
Again, I'm so sorry.
-A

Allison,
Considering you haven't taken a night off in three years, yes. I believe we can make that work. I'll have some of my office staff clean up. Please don't trouble yourself about it, and have a very well-deserved break.
-Doctor Roth

sixteen

ADINA

"YOU'RE DOING A GREAT JOB, ADINA."

I'm trying not to look too pleased with myself, but I might be fighting a losing battle. After all, social work is all I've wanted to do... forever. Well, not forever, but definitely since I grew out of the angry teenager that I was and decided to take a stab at living a normal life. Maybe it would seem crazy to some people that I was running right back into the world I so narrowly escaped, but it just felt... right.

I want to help kids like me; kids who might not have had the easiest start to life, but still deserve every opportunity to live. Not every lost girl has an Asher Roth and, despite how rough I've had it, I've never taken for granted how lucky I was. My story could have gone very differently, and if I can help just one other kid... well. Maybe working through my shit will be worth it.

It's one thing to think all that, though, and it's another for your internship supervisor to pull you into her office to praise your work for twenty minutes straight.

Pressing my lips together to keep myself from beaming, I nod very professionally. "Thanks so much, Faith."

Faith's office is tiny and cluttered, her windowless walls clustered with framed certificates and colorful hand-drawn pictures. There's a stack of files on her desk that's probably taller than I am, and there's a coffee stain on the front of her blouse. Still, she's smiling warmly at me, and the research report I spent weeks slaving over is sitting in front of her, covered in highlighter marks.

"This really is good stuff." She indicates the stapled packet. "I'm impressed. Do you have any plans for after you graduate?"

My stomach flips. "I, ah, always wanted to work here. As a caseworker." I say it a little sheepishly, still half expecting her to laugh in my face. The Department of Child Welfare isn't exactly well funded, and most of the people in this department have worked here for decades. I'm one of five interns right now, and the others go to way better colleges than I do.

Faith doesn't laugh, though. On the contrary, she leans back in her swivel chair, regarding me appraisingly. "I think you have a very good shot of that. Full-time positions are hard to come by at first, especially right out of college, but if you can stick it out through a per diem period, you'd be first in line." She smiles apologetically. "Do you mind me asking what your living situation is? It can be tough living in the city."

I bite my lip. I haven't moved in with Asher, not *officially*, but I also haven't spent a single night on the couch since we first slept together a week ago. Even if all I see of him is when I'm crawling into his bed past midnight, bone-tired and starving after racing from my internship to the coffee shop and then to his office to clean before finally dragging my sore feet to his apartment. The whole double-life thing is wearing on me, and I know I need to tell him that last—admittedly huge—piece of the puzzle soon.

"I think I'm going to be moving in with my boyfriend soon," I admit sheepishly, even though saying it out loud feels like tempting fate. We're happy, but that could change. As impossibly painful as it is to consider, I could lose him, and it would be no one's fault but my own.

Faith nods cheerfully, oblivious to my sudden worry. "Well, good work. Keep doing what you're doing. I'll put a letter of recommendation in your file that should help a lot come hiring time." She winks. "Tell Gina in HR that she still owes me that favor."

* * *

Asher is waiting outside the DCW building when I step outside. He's leaning back on a bench with his hands shoved in his pockets, looking even more handsome than usual in an ironed shirt and the same bow tie he wore the night we met at The Witt.

My heart flips as he stands, strolling toward me with all the confidence of a man who *knows* I'm gone for him. I've barely managed a soft hello before he plants a hand on the small of my back and drags my body into his, lips descending on mine in a kiss that makes my head spin.

"Hi," I say again when we break apart, blinking dazedly up at him. It's not even five, the sky is still blue, and tonight I am going on my very first date. Ever. I'm also trying not to get ahead of myself—because clearly there are obstacles ahead—but this had better be my *last* first date.

The corner of Asher's lips lift into a crooked smile as he

steps back to look me up and down. "You're so beautiful, angel."

Normally, I'd think he's being generous, but I *do* look pretty good. This morning I went to a discount department store in between classes and panic bought a neat skirt and blouse that was appropriate for my internship and tonight's date. Before I left the building, I took my hair down from the braided bun I'd worn it in all day, and now it's perfectly wavy without a hint of frizz. I'm taking it as a good omen.

"You are too. Handsome, I mean." My hands move to his bow tie, adjusting it as I feel my face split in a smile of my own.

Asher's smile widens as he pulls me out of the way of a group of tourists who are taking up the better part of the sidewalk. "Are you ready to be romanced within an inch of your life?"

"I'm not sure. Sounds dangerous," I quip smoothly, lacing my fingers through his. It feels natural now, like we've been doing it for years instead of weeks. Something brings me up short, though, and I lift our twined hands, staring at the bandage wrapped around Asher's right index finger. "What happened?"

He rolls his eyes, letting our hands fall as we set off along the sidewalk. "A five-year-old bit me."

My jaw drops. "That *happens*?" I squeak, immediately alarmed.

"Not often, thankfully." Asher chuckles, unphased. "It's not bad. Her mother was mortified, though. The incident was more traumatic for her than it was for me."

I shudder, squeezing his hand. "I'm very glad I chose social work right about now."

He doesn't respond to that, and when I peek up at him, I can see the unspoken question in his face.

"I'll tell you the whole story someday," I assure him gently, even though my heart pangs because I'm ready to tell him *now*. There's no way to tell him the whole truth though, not without revealing that *he* is a big part of why I chose this path. I know I need to tell him... It's officially been too long and I'm so tired of this massive, horrible secret hanging over me. Sometimes it's all I can think about, and twice in the past week I've woken up from dreams of Asher telling me he never wants to see me again, gasping for air and damp with sweat.

Undoubtedly able to sense my plummeting mood, Asher tucks me under his arm and presses a kiss to the crown of my hair. "I love you."

Just like that, I melt.

"I love you too," I murmur, my heart lifting as I look up at him. "Will you tell me where you're taking me? Or will that interfere with the high level of romancing that you're aiming for?"

His lips quirk in a wry smile. "No interference. Come on, let's get a car and I'll tell you on the way." He steps to the curb and raises his hand, hailing a cab. When the man pulls over, he opens the door for me. It's old fashioned, but something about the gesture makes me stop in my tracks, staring at him. There are probably big cartoon hearts pulsing in my eyes right now, because—even after the onslaught of romantic gestures this man has already thrown down in his pursuit to win me over—I swear I've never felt so much for anyone or anything than I do right now.

"Adina?"

I blink, shaking myself from my love-struck daze, and hurry to fold myself into the back seat of the car. Asher follows, rattling off an address I don't recognize to the driver, who grunts his acknowledgement before pulling out into traffic.

"Want to tell me what that was back there?" He murmurs in my ear, wrapping an arm around my shoulders and kissing my temple.

Sighing, I lean into the warmth of his chest, my eyes on the darkening city beyond the windshield of the car. "I'm just happy."

I wish I could bottle this feeling and store it away for when I need it most.

Asher hums. "That was the goal. If I'd known you'd be happy with a cab ride, I would have done this sooner."

He's joking, but I really would be happy just going for a drive with him. Or cuddling on the couch in his apartment watching movies. Or holding his hand to walk to the store. I swallow the lump in my throat and peer up at him. "You know, you don't have to do all this for me. I'm not—I mean, I really am happy just being with you."

He stares back at me for a long moment, and there's something raw and new in his expression that I've never seen there before. "You deserve to be treated like this, Adina. You're the best thing that's ever happened to me, and the day I take that for granted is the day you leave my ass. Do you understand?" My bottom lip trembles, and he smooths his thumb over it, his expression soft. "You've been so strong for so long, angel. I know there are things you haven't told me, that you might *never* tell me, but you're not on your own anymore."

I don't respond. I can't.

All I can do is wrap myself around him and rest my head on his shoulder as the city flashes by outside the cab.

No more putting it off. We'll have tonight, and then tomorrow... Tomorrow, after work, I'll tell him everything.

Tomorrow.

seventeen

ASHER

IN THE SEVEN months since I came home to find my girlfriend gone, my apartment all but emptied out, and everything I thought I wanted in ruins, I've become a different person.

Far from the man who was gripped by cold, gnawing panic at the thought of committing to one woman for the rest of his life, I've found myself browsing engagement rings online during lunch breaks and wondering if I could make room in my scant budget to surprise Adina with a honeymoon. *Goddamn*, I'd love to see her ass in a bikini.

It's too soon—*far* too soon—but I can't help the gnawing suspicion that Adina would thrive in the stability and permanence of marriage. We've come such a long way in such a short amount of time, but that fear in her eyes is still present, particularly when we're at our happiest. It's like she thinks it's all going to be ripped away, and while it's gut wrenching, how could I blame her?

Last night, I took her to a modern art installation. We spent hours wandering amidst massive technicolor sculptures and through structures made entirely of light. In truth, I could only describe about half of what we saw. I was too busy enjoying Adina's reactions, obsessed with the way she would automatically look to me whenever there was something particularly exciting or beautiful. Afterward, we stopped at the same Mexican restaurant we discovered on that first night, talking about our days.

It was incredible.

Not quite as incredible as later, though, when we got home and she rode my cock on the living room floor.

Sex with Adina is better than anything I've ever experienced. After weeks of buildup, of eating her pussy and fisting my own cock to relieve some of the tension, our first night together was fucking transcendent. Not just the physical intimacy, but also the knowledge that I understand this woman better than anyone else on Earth. I know she's *mine*, and while we still have a long way to go, I'm equally sure we'll figure it out.

It's startling to look back at the years I spent in my former relationship through this new lens, one that sheds a stark, unflattering light on how unhappy we were. There was no laughter or joy in our home, sex was routine and perfunctory, and, often, even the smallest decisions turned to fights.

When Lindsey left, that was just... it. We were done, and it was time to move on. Or, in my case, despise myself for not being able to make something work that wasn't right to begin with. There were no drunken, pleading voicemails, or angry, emotional talks. After six years together, we didn't even say goodbye. I expected her to reach out, if only to have the last word, but it never happened. As the months have passed, I stopped expecting her to.

Today, with fresh memories of my beautiful girlfriend writhing on top of me, tits bouncing as she rides me into oblivion... well. Needless to say, there isn't another woman on my mind. Why would I be dwelling on the past when my future is here and it's more than I ever knew to hope for? Adina won't be in until late tonight, which gives me time to make—or at least make a passable attempt at—dinner and plan my next great objective: getting her to move in with me. There are only a few more months left of her final semester at school. She'll be taking her first steps into her future, and there isn't a doubt in my mind that I want to be by her side.

Now, I just need to convince her.

At last, when the day finally drags to a close, I'm just at the point of gathering my things when there's a short knock. June, my receptionist, pokes her head in, looking apprehensive.

I still, staring at her in some alarm. "Everything okay?"

June makes a face. "Yeah, we're good. Everyone's heading out. But, um, *Lindsey* is here to see you. I said I'd have to check if you were still here. Want me to get rid of her?" It couldn't be clearer by the way she says my ex-girl-friend's name that she doesn't approve.

Lindsey is here?

Swallowing back my shock, I shake my head. "No. Have her wait. I'll be right there."

With one last disapproving *humph*, June vanishes. I stand stock-still, staring blankly at the back of the door. It's been seven months, and I can't imagine what she'd want now. Unless... *Shit.* Her mom has been sick for ages. If she's passed, if Lindsey wants me to go to the funeral, I have no idea how I'll handle it. The woman didn't even like me, surely she'd be perfectly fine without me standing awkwardly amidst the mourners at her funeral.

There's no time to think about it.

I find my ex-girlfriend waiting in the empty lobby. Her hands are folded neatly in her lap, and she's staring at the mural of dancing teeth like they've offended her somehow. Since I last saw her, she's obviously undergone something of a reinvention. Her hair is lighter, her skin is tanner, and her clothes seem more trendy than what she wore when we were together. She's still Lindsey, though, the same woman I slept beside for six years, and staring at her now... I feel nothing.

"Asher." Her eyes narrow on me as she stands, adjusting the strap of her handbag on her shoulder.

What do I say to her? I swallow. "What are you doing here?"

Her lips flatten into a line. "Can we speak privately?" She glances around the waiting room, again with that same air of disdain. There's nobody here—undoubtedly June left for the night after informing me of Lindsey's arrival—but I don't argue. Without another word, I turn back the way I came and lead the way to my office. By the time I've turned, leaning back against my desk, she's closing the door behind her.

"What's this about?"

For a moment, Lindsey just stares at me. Then, scathingly, she says, "I know."

"Know?"

"Yes." Her lip curls. "I'm doing *fine* without you, Asher. Great, even. I'm seeing someone, and it's going very well. In fact, he took me to the Nona exhibit last night. Have you been?"

My stomach drops. *Christ.* She saw Adina and me together at the museum. I should be sorry that it's obviously upset her, but I can't bring myself to care. "We've been broken up for *months*, Lindsey. You said yourself that you're seeing someone. What does it matter if I am?"

Across the small office, Lindsey looks murderous. "Do you think I'm stupid?"

"For fuck's sake—"

"No!" Her voice has risen now, and she steps forward, chest heaving. "You were cheating on me. That's why you didn't want to get married, why you were always at work. That's why you didn't even bother to make sure I was okay after I left. You had a hot, young replacement lined up."

My jaw goes slack. "I met her six weeks ago. Not even, actually. This is ridiculous. Please leave."

Lindsey's fists curl at her sides, and she looks so furious, I think for a moment that she might actually hit me. Former relationship or not, if she takes one more step toward me, I'm calling the police. "You're such a liar," she snarls, and steps back toward the hall. "Put on whatever good-guy pretense you want, Asher, but I know the truth. That's all I came here to say. I hope you and your precious *Allison* are very happy together."

I still, gazing at her. "Why would you—what makes you think the woman I was with last night is Allison?"

Lindsey scoffs. "I told you I wasn't stupid. Did you seriously think your girlfriend would just blindly accept you were letting some random teenager sleep in your office without getting suspicious? I saw her there one night, you *asshole*. I sat right outside your office and watched her go in." She snorts, turning to go. "Silly me. I thought you wouldn't be interested in a trashy little street rat. Apparently, I overestimated your standards."

Without another word, she flings open the door and storms out of sight.

My hands find the desk behind me, the wood biting into

my palms as I stare unseeingly at the worn office couch across from me. The couch where Allison has curled up to sleep every night for three years.

I can't move.

I can barely breathe.

Lindsey has to be wrong. It must be years since she's seen Allison... She's remembering wrong. There's no way.

But almost as soon as I've dismissed it, I realize I can't.

Adina's late nights working, the scent of cleaners in her hair, the things she's told me about her past... It fits. I don't want it to, but my personal feelings don't change the facts. Like it or not, and as ugly as it is to admit, I know frighteningly little about the woman I've fallen in love with. The first night we slept together, I'd known there was more to the story. When she hadn't continued, though, I wrote it off as being too much for her. I was so blinded by my feelings, so horrified by what she'd told me and simultaneously thrilled that she'd finally opened up...

It's kept me up for years, the memory of that stoic girl with her beaten face, totally prepared to die in the cold. I'd felt confident that what I did to help her was enough and that she would move on to bigger and better things. The notes she'd left me, the little hints she's been doing better —my stomach churns—that she was in college now.

Swallowing back the bitter taste of bile, I turn, looking frantically to the door of the closet where I've let Allison store her things. Never in the three years she's been here have I been tempted to invade her privacy. Now, though... I push off the desk, moving forward, even as my mind remains scrambling to find a way around all this.

Lindsey was wrong. *I* am wrong. This is a bizarre coincidence, it has to be, because the alternative... I'm not sure I could live with myself.

My chest is tight as I open the door, staring down at the lime-green bin pushed neatly off in the corner. Dropping to my knees, I drag it toward me. It's not heavy or particularly large, yet my muscles protest with the effort it takes to lift the lid.

Before I've even glimpsed the contents, I *know*.

The scent of honey and wildflowers assaults my senses, an indisputable, agonizing confirmation of what Lindsey revealed. Was it only a few minutes ago that she stormed out of here? It feels like hours have passed, days even. Yet again, Adina Collier has turned my life upside down, and this time... I press my hand to my mouth, shuddering as the lid clatters to the ground beside me.

The contents of the box are neatly organized. A plastic bag of what must be laundry is shoved in the furthest corner, beside another of neatly folded clean clothes. There are tiny bottles of travel shampoo, a toothbrush and tooth-paste, a few college textbooks, and a phone charger. An entire life, crammed into a fucking box.

Numbly, I reach out to touch the T-shirt on top of the pile of clothing. It's worn and faded with age, with a small hole just below the neckline from when I caught it on a lamp while moving. The same one I dressed her in that very first morning at The Witt.

My eyes catch on the one item which seems unessen-tial: a small, stained-glass box. It's resting neatly atop the textbooks, as though she opens it regularly. Knowing that what I find in it couldn't possibly make me feel more terrible than I do already, I open that too.

Notes.

Hundreds of notes, all in my handwriting. They are, by the look of it, every single word I've ever written to Allison.

Not Allison—*Adina*—because of course she would have

signed that first note with a fake name. She'd run away before and was taken back, wasn't she? There's no way she would have risked it again.

Which means that my angel, the woman I love, has been sleeping on a fucking couch for three years. She's been scrubbing the fucking toilets at my practice, then dragging herself back across town to sleep in my arms. She's been storing everything she owns in a plastic tote bin, shoved in the back of my closet. All while I slept soundly, feeling *good* about what I did for Allison.

Now—*fuck*—the horrible things I'd imagined about her former life aren't imagined anymore. I saw evidence of them three years ago. With my own eyes, I saw her bruises, her brutally cut hair, and the cold, grim acceptance with which she faced almost certain death.

The noise I make is like that of a wounded animal, and I stumble back to my feet, trying to put as much distance as possible between myself and the box. Like if I can't see the evidence, I'll be able to deny what I already know. It's impossible. Every second that passes only brings more questions and horrible realizations.

It all fits. From that first night at The Witt, I felt drawn to her, like we'd known each other for a long time—*because we have*. Allison was my friend long before Adina became my lover.

How could she not have told me?

ADINA

IT TAKES AN EXTRA-LARGE COFFEE, one mental pep talk, and an accidental nap on the subway to get me to Asher's practice tonight.

I'm so tired, my whole body hurts, and my vision is starting to do that weird buzzy thing around the edges. Apparently, adding 'girlfriend' to my schedule hasn't helped the whole sleep-deprivation situation. Though sleeping in Asher's bed has been way better than the couch in his office, and cutting out showering at the gym has helped a bit. Even my academic standards have slipped a little in the past few weeks. I'm doing well, nothing to be concerned about, but I'm not circling every extra credit assignment like a fish going after a worm.

Ruby, who definitely knows I'm still seeing Asher but refuses to acknowledge it in any way, claims I have "senior slack-off syndrome," and she's not wrong. I've never been one of those people who loves school—it has always been a means to an end—and now that the end is nearly reached... Well, I'm out and excited to never open another textbook for the rest of my life.

My distraction isn't just due to "senior slack- off syndrome," though. Not today. Instead of taking notes in my trauma psychology course, I spent the entire seminar writing out a speech to Asher, confessing that I'm Allison. By the end, I had something I was *almost* happy with. Obviously, I'm not going to stand there reading it in front of him, but hopefully I can at least look it over one more time before getting to his apartment tonight. Because I *will* be telling him tonight. No more excuses. No more putting it off.

I have no idea how he's going to react, and I'm still not sure if it would have been better to have told him at the start of this. It would have been easier to write this off as a wild coincidence, maybe, but if I'd done that, would he have fallen in love with me? Or would he have always seen me as poor runaway Allison, curled up beside the trash bins?

I thought he'd wanted something casual, and thought if that was all of him I could get, then I'd better take it. After all, my feelings for Asher go back so much further than his feelings for me. It was so selfish, but I've never wanted anything more than I wanted him. I think a part of me hoped that if this romance business didn't work out, at least I'd still have him as a friend.

He'll understand. He might be angry, but... *God.* I hope he understands.

It's almost nine at night by the time I make it down the deserted street where Asher and I first met. I've spent so much time here over the last few years that this neighborhood is more familiar to me than anywhere else on Earth. I don't even have to take my keys out of my pocket to find the one I need, slightly longer than the few others, and it turns easily in the practice's door. Everything about this is routine, but as I move to disarm the alarm system, I still.

It isn't set.

I swallow, turning to face the empty waiting room. It's still and quiet, the usual jumble of coloring books and broken crayons are scattered over on the long, narrow coffee table, and the little wastepaper bin beside the coffee machine is overflowing. Beyond the long, curved reception desk, the computers are powered down, and lights from a passing car shine brightly through the blinds.

Everything is normal, but not once in three years has Asher forgotten to set the alarm. Now, the tiny hairs on the back of my neck are standing on end.

My hand closes around the little pepper spray canister hanging from my keychain as I edge further into the building, listening for signs of an intruder. The practice is quiet, though, and even the muted rumble of traffic fades as I move into the hall which leads to the cleaning chairs and offices.

I'm being ridiculous. There's no one here. Asher forgot to set the alarm because he, like me, spent the better part of last night having sex.

Gusting out a long sigh, I trudge forward, still grasping the pepper spray but not expecting to encounter anyone. There's a safe used to store narcotics just off the room with all the equipment sterilizers, and a quick peek confirms it's untouched. Surely if someone were to break in, they wouldn't have locked the front door behind them, and that safe would have been their first target. I doubt the criminals of New York are particularly interested in Asher's old desktop computer or tooth-extraction equipment.

As I push open the door to his office, though, already slinging my too heavy backpack over my shoulder, I let out a high-pitched, shrill scream. There, leaning against the desk in the center of the dimly lit room, is a tall, broad-shouldered man.

I'm only terrified for a second, though. Or, at least, I'm only afraid some petty criminal is about to whack me over the head for a second.

Then, the fear becomes something else entirely.

"Asher." My voice breaks, and I fumble with the light switch, realizing half a second too late that I'm not sure I want to see his face right now.

Through all this, he hasn't moved a muscle, and as the overhead fluorescent lights flicker to life, it's all I can do to keep my legs from collapsing beneath me.

The man I love is staring at the floor, his expression set and stony. He looks... He looks colder than I've ever seen him, like all the light has gone out behind his eyes. Behind him, the door to the closet is open and my green storage bin is sitting in the doorway, its lid cast aside.

No. Please no.

Somehow, I never imagined him finding out like this. In all the different ways I've played out this conversation in my head, I was never *caught*. All the careful words I'd tried to memorize are thrown to the wind, lost. They don't matter anymore.

My eyes sting, and a ragged sob breaks free from my lips. "Asher, please—"

"*Don't*. Don't talk right now, Adina."

Something shatters deep inside me. I think it might be my heart.

My bottom lip trembles as I reach into my pocket, pulling out the folded note I'd written during my seminar. Only a few minutes ago, I had hoped it would be enough, but not anymore.

Asher doesn't look at me as I approach, gently setting it on the desk beside him. God, this hurts so bad. I always thought "broken heart" was an expression, but it's not, because I *feel* broken.

Still, as I step back toward the door, I can't help hoping that he'll call out and stop me. He doesn't. Of course he doesn't, because why would he? As if this man wasn't spectacularly out of my league before, now he knows I'm a fraud too. A stupid, damaged girl who fell in love with a man that she neglected common sense, and now she'll be right back to where she started. Homeless and alone.

I hover at the edge of the room, and it's an effort just to open my mouth and speak. "I'll go," I whisper, barely audible.

At my words, Asher's head snaps up, and he stares at me through narrowed eyes. "What the hell does that mean?" he demands savagely, and I pause, confusion cutting uncomfortably into my grief.

I blink. "I thought... I mean..."

His eyes flash behind his glasses. "You thought I'd want you gone? That I'd throw you out on the street in fucking February? Is that why you didn't tell me?"

My mouth pops open, but all I can manage is a choked noise of disbelief.

Asher growls, cursing under his breath, and points at the couch. "Sit, Adina. *Sit there*, and don't fucking move."

He doesn't want me to leave? That's something, isn't it? If he were ending this, he'd just want me to go, right?

I sit, watching as Asher begins to pace the room, his long legs carrying him from one wall to another. He's like a caged animal, and I don't know what I'm supposed to be doing with myself. Do I try to say something?

"Asher—"

"No."

Okay, then.

My tears are still falling, but as I huddle in the corner of the couch, I can't help thinking that *maybe* this isn't totally hopeless. Asher seems to be working through this in his own way, and apparently he just wants me to sit here and watch him do it. Fair enough. I got us into this mess and, exhausted or not, I'll sit here all night if it means I won't lose him over it.

At some point, Asher seems to become aware of the note I left. He pauses in front of his desk, staring at it, before setting off again.

After at least fifteen minutes of continuous pacing, I'm practically bursting with the need to say something. I'm not even crying anymore, but the brand-new wound inside me throbs painfully. Even though he hasn't thrown me out, that doesn't mean he wants to work this out or that he'll ever forgive me. I should be grateful that I might not lose my place to live, but I think curling up on this couch again after knowing what it's like to sleep in Asher's arms— knowing he doesn't want me anymore and is counting down the days until I graduate and leave—would be a special kind of torture.

I'm just working up the nerve to say something when, out of nowhere, he stops again, eyes on the folded note. I hadn't written it for him to read, but it's proof at least that I've wanted to tell him, that I *planned* to tell him. For a moment, I think he's just going to stare at it again, but my heart leaps into my throat when he picks it up.

He doesn't look at me or acknowledge me in any way, but slowly Asher begins to unfold the note.

I'm not sure I've ever felt so helpless. My whole heart is poured onto that one page of ripped notebook paper. The way I feel about him, the way I've *always* felt about him, the reasons why I didn't tell him sooner, and what I want for our future—it's all there.

Asher's eyes fly back and forth over the note, his brow furrowed and mouth set into a flat line. Once or twice, I see him stop and close his eyes like he needs to steady himself before beginning again. It's torture, sitting here and watching as he decides whether all of it is good enough. There are other things I should have said. Maybe if I'd used different words, explained differently...

My mouth goes dry when, finally, Asher's hand falls. The note drops back onto his desk, and the unearthly stillness and quiet of the empty practice presses in on us. He turns to me, lifting his eyes to meet mine, and *I don't know what to do*. I have no idea how to make up with someone, or repair a relationship I've fucked up, or even break this awful, everlasting silence.

"I understand why you didn't tell me."

What?

I make a quiet, helpless noise of shocked disbelief, gazing up at him through wide eyes. Since I walked into this room, a million horrible possibilities of how this could end have gone through my mind, and none of them involved Asher calmly accepting what I'd done. I'm utterly unprepared, and now that it finally seems like it's okay for me to speak, I'm lost for words.

Asher rakes a hand through his hair, throat bobbing. "I know that you trust me—that you love me—but given your history, how could I have expected you to risk the security you have here?" His voice is quiet and sad as he gestures vaguely at the room we're in. "To be honest, I have no idea what I would have done if I was in your position."

Tears blur my vision. I try to speak again, but the words

are nowhere to be found. This can't actually be happening, can it? He can't just... forgive me?

Like he knows what I'm thinking, the corner of Asher's lips lift in a pained, humorless smile. "Did you actually believe I would throw you out?"

My throat tightens, because *yeah*, I kind of did. "I'm used to being alone. I've never had... *people*." My voice is hollow. "I didn't know."

Asher's shoulders sag, and he moves toward me, finally stopping just before me. He sinks to his knees at my feet, and I think my heart might be breaking for a whole different reason now as he takes my hands in his. "Listen to me," he murmurs gently. "I'm not going anywhere. *Ever*, Adina. This is it for me. You are the hardest working, kindest, most beautiful person I've ever known. I am in awe of you every single day, and being the first person to love you the way you deserve is the greatest privilege of my life."

I break.

One moment I'm staring at him, hope and shame brimming inside me, and the next I'm sobbing.

Asher holds me close, his lips pressed to my temple and big hand stroking reassuringly up and down my spine. "I'm sorry," I blubber over and over again, but he just shakes his head.

"We're going to be alright, angel." He gathers my face in his hands, forcing me to meet his eyes. I must look horrible, my eyes shadowed with exhaustion and shining with tears, but he looks at me like I'm the most beautiful thing he's ever seen. "I do have some requests. Three, actually."

I'm nodding before he finishes the sentence. "Anything." It's true. I would do anything for this man, and I'm not afraid of feeling that way anymore.

Thumbs swipe over my cheeks, wiping away the

remaining tears, and Asher smiles gently at me. "Firstly, you're going to move in with me. *Tonight.* I can't stomach the thought of you sleeping on this fucking couch one more time."

For all he said about this being a request, it sure sounds like demand. It seems stupid to say no when I *want* that. My head bobs up and down in silent agreement, and some of the tension seems to bleed from Asher's shoulders.

"Secondly"—he throws me a warning look that suggests this next request won't be so easy for me to to accept—"you won't clean this office anymore. The coffee shop I can stomach—barely—but I won't have you on your hands and knees scrubbing the fucking toilets after all you do during the day."

I swallow, wracking my brain for how I could possibly make this work with my already razor-thin budget. My expenses are fairly low, especially now that I won't have books and school fees to pay for, and if I'm going to be living with Asher, I wouldn't have to keep saving for an apartment. "How much is half the rent at your apartment?" I ask quietly, even though it seems like such a stupid thing to be asking after such an emotional night.

Asher scowls. "You're not paying rent, Adina." He sounds appalled that I even suggested it. "I'm not going to ask you to give up a free place to live, then expect hundreds of extra dollars a month out of you for rent." Hundreds seems pretty generous, considering the city we live in. Even Asher's apartment, which is small and not in the best neighborhood, must cost thousands.

I bite my lip. "I don't want to take advantage—"

"You're *not*," he bites out impatiently, his hands holding my face a little tighter. "I want to take care of you, and more than that, I want you to feel safe. Tomorrow morning, I'll call the landlord and make sure your name is added to the lease. If it makes you happy, you can start paying rent when you graduate."

How could he know how badly I've needed that security?

My eyes blur with tears again, but I fight them off as I nod once more, my heart so full it could burst. How is it possible to go from total devastation to complete joy in such a short period of time? It doesn't seem possible.

Asher makes a small, relieved noise, and then he's leaning forward, kissing me fiercely.

"What's request number three?" I ask with a shaky laugh when we break apart, panting.

Asher is already rolling to his feet, though, and I watch as he crosses the room to press the lid back on the green bin and lift it up under his arm.

"We'll talk about it tomorrow." He stops beside me and holds out his free hand. "Come on, angel. Let's go home."

As I take it, it occurs to me that I've been waiting a long time—twenty-one years, actually—for someone to say that to me.

Asher,

To be honest, I have no idea how to start this, so I guess I'll just... start.

When I told you about my past the other night, there were important things I left out.
The truth is that the night at The Witt wasn't the first time we've met. I knew who you were because three years ago, you saved my life.

After running away the second time and hitting brick walls every way I turned, I wanted to give up. I was walking down the sidewalk, and I just stopped by these trash cans and sat down. I didn't move for hours. People averted their eyes and nobody spoke to me, and it was like every single one of them was further proving that I was worth nothing. Except you.
I'm so sorry I lied to you. First by signing those notes as Allison, and then not telling you right away.
A little piece of me fell in love with you that first...

night on the street. Over the years, as I learned more about you, I just kept falling harder. When we came face-to-face in The Witt, it pretty much sealed the deal for me. I wanted as much of you as I could get, even if it was just for one night.

I trust you more than anyone else in this world, and I'm still terrified that you knowing there are darker parts of me will send you running for the hills. I'm not trying to make excuses, but that's the truth.

There are a lot of reasons I didn't tell you, and reasons I allowed myself to keep putting this conversation off. We can talk about them if you want, but in retrospect they seem pretty flimsy. Hopefully I can make them sound as convincing as they did in my head before I actually tell you all this.

Today. I'm telling you today.

I love you so much.

—Adina

nineteen

ASHER

BY THE TIME we made it home, Adina was so exhausted that she'd barely been able to take off her own shoes.

For the second time in one night, I knelt at her feet. She held my shoulders, allowing me to unlace her boots and chuck them into a pile with my own beside the front door. I hadn't stopped at the shoes. I'd stripped her clothes off right there in the entryway, pressing chaste, lingering kisses over every new patch of exposed skin.

She'd hummed contentedly when I lifted her into my arms, pressing her face into my neck as I strode through to the bedroom. We'd never made the bed that morning, and it was strange to set her down in the same spot we'd had sleepy, slow sex only hours ago.

The room was the same, but we were different.

My poor girl. Every time my mind returns to what she's been through, the brand new wound inside me seems to tear open all over again.

I *hate* the thought of her feeling like a liar and a fraud for protecting herself.

I hate the thought of her curled up alone on that fucking couch night after night.

There are a million things about this that turn my stomach. The thing I hate worst of all, though, the thing that kept me up half the night, is the memory of Adina the night we met—the *real* night we met.

When I told her I was in awe of her, it was an understatement. That the broken, lost girl by the trash could grow to be the intelligent, kind, and elegant woman I'd fallen so madly in love with... *Christ*, it seems impossible.

Maybe that's why I never put the pieces of the puzzle together myself. How could *anyone* get the very worst life has to offer before they're even old enough to vote, yet still choose to give back to the world? How is it possible that despite everything she's been through, my angel isn't cynical, angry, or cold?

Somewhere over the course of the evening, something fundamental changed in me. It seems almost comical that only yesterday I thought there was no possible way for me to fall harder for Adina Collier, when now... Well, now, I doubt there's a part of my heart that this woman doesn't own completely.

I haven't forgotten that she turned down three thousand dollars out of respect for me, even when she was sleeping on a couch and working her fingers to the bone. How could any man on this Earth be luckier than I am?

She'd gazed up at me through the darkness as I pulled off my own clothes, and I'd barely laid down before she was curled against me. I held her close until the tension slowly faded from her muscles and her breaths became long and even.

It took me much longer to fall asleep, but when I finally

did, I was plagued by nightmares of snowstorms and Adina's tears.

I give up on getting a full night's sleep before the sun has risen, but I'm grateful for the time to think. My third request, the one I have serious doubts she'll actually agree to, is going to require a longer conversation. I'm still trying to think of a good way to approach it when daylight begins to filter in through the blinds, and the woman I love stirs in my arms, making a soft, sleepy noise of contentment.

"Hi," she murmurs, fingers skimming absently through my chest hair as I reach for my glasses on the bedside table. This is a conversation I'd like to see her properly for.

"Good morning." I settle back, gazing at her. She still looks tired, but better than last night. There's something else in her face, though, something I'm not sure I've seen there before.

Hope.

Maybe when she hears my third request, that will turn to plain optimism.

Adina bites her lip. "No regrets?" Her eyes flit to the corner of the room where I left her storage bin last night.

I let out a short, disbelieving laugh. "Hell, no. Do you? It occurred to me after you fell asleep that I may have exploited this situation to my advantage."

My words are met by a lazy, mischievous smirk. With a teasing little tug, Adina shifts the bedding so I can see the entire length of her bare body.

I groan as she makes a show of getting on her hands and knees and crawling until her body is over mine. I'm dressed only in a pair of boxers, and I wasn't hard mere seconds ago. The sight of her tight, perky breasts in my face, though, is all it takes to turn my cock to stone.

Adina settles back in my lap, her bare sex pressed right

over my length, separated by a thin layer of cotton. I can feel the heat coming off her, feel how slick she's gotten. She rocks over my shaft, nipples pebbling in the drafty apartment air, and I let my head drop back into the pillow, enjoying her little performance.

Normally, I'd let her play for as long as she likes, but today? *Goddamn.* I need to get inside her.

I grit my teeth. "Do you want to play, angel? Or do you want to give me what I want?"

There's a soft inhale of shock at those words, and that's all it takes. She lifts her hips, allowing me to tug my boxers down and grip my shaft, aligning it with her hot, wet entrance.

"Sit."

Watching her do this is always a reminder of how mismatched in size we are. I'm nearly a foot taller than she is and have a dick to match. It's perverse, but I can't lie to myself. There's nothing more satisfying than stretching her body to fit mine.

We've been fucking for weeks now, but her eyebrows still knit together with worry when she gets the first half of me. It's a reminder of what a filthy, old man I am, how much I love that I'm too big for my twenty-one-year-old girlfriend's tight pussy.

She's determined today, and doesn't falter as she lowers herself over me, impaling herself on my dick.

Like she's thinking along the same lines I am, Adina's lips fall open in a quiet sigh when her ass finally settles in my lap. "Does it feel good, daddy?"

Fuck yeah, it does.

I hum my approval, careful to keep my expression unimpressed. My girl loves to hear what she does to me, but these last weeks have taught me that she gets so much wetter and comes so much harder when she earns her praise. "Sure does. I think you know how you could make me feel better, though."

A fresh wave of sticky arousal coats my dick, and Adina hesitates for all of half a second before she's lifting onto her knees and shoving herself back down. Soft, breathy whimpers fill the room as my girl bounces on top of me, her hands planted on my chest and her back arched to give me a better view of her tits.

"Going to make yourself come?" I ask with a throaty chuckle, running my hands over her hips. My balls are already tight and aching, ready to blow, but it's always like that when I fuck her. Even if she made me come an hour ago, the moment I get inside her tight cunt, it's a battle to keep myself from spilling too soon.

Fingers digging into my chest, Adina rocks over me, faster and faster. Her mouth pops open, and I expect her to moan or beg, but what she says instead fucking rocks me.

"I love you."

Goddamn it. This woman.

With a groan, I reach up to pull her close and push us both over, sealing her between my body and the mattress. "I love you too, angel. So much. Fuck me, this feels good. Your little hole is a goddamn miracle, making me feel so good—" Fresh wetness coats my length, and it snaps the invisible tether keeping me in control.

The noise I make is one of pure animalistic desire. My abs strain and my thighs burn as I let loose, pumping my cock into that intensely narrow channel as hard as I can until Adina's legs shake and her back bows off the bed.

"Daddy!"

I'll never get tired of hearing her call me that when she's coming. "Do you want my cum?" I grunt, shifting my weight to one arm so I can cradle one of her tits in my hand, kneading and squeezing. There's no finesse to it, just raw need to make sure she feels me *everywhere*. "Tell me, angel."

"Yeah—oh, fuck—yes!" She hiccups, clutching my shoulders as the last of her orgasm dies away.

I grit my teeth, bearing down harder as heat begins to build at the base of my spine. I'm desperate to come now, aching to shoot my load so deep it leaks out of her for hours. If today goes as planned—if she agrees to my third request—she's going to have a piece of me inside her when we do it.

I want to be connected to this woman, joined in every biological, emotional, and legal way possible.

Adina's heels lock behind my back, her cries sounding in my ear as she tries to drag me closer.

"Here it comes," I grit out, my pace faltering as I press my face into her neck, greedily inhaling my favorite scent.

I come violently and without warning. My vision goes black as pleasure explodes within me, making my whole body shake with the force of it as I unload deep inside her. I have no idea how long it goes on or how long I lay on top of her, unable to bring myself to pull away.

When the sweat has begun to cool on my back and I'm positive my muscles are about to give way, I fall to her side with a weak laugh. Soft hands stroke gently through my hair as I recover, our limbs tangled beneath the covers. My boxers have somehow become tangled around one of my legs, but my cock is out, a combination of our releases drying on my skin. It's imperfect and intimate, and fucking incredible.

There's only one thing that could possibly motivate me to move.

"We have to get going," I mumble, lifting my head to check the time on the alarm clock.

Adina blinks, watching with confusion as I roll out of bed and stride to the small closet in the corner. "Where?"

I wish I had more time to plan this. Adina deserves a hell of a lot more than to rush it, but I don't want to leave her feeling the slightest bit unsettled for even a few more hours. After she fell asleep last night, I booked the earliest appointment available and texted Liam to call in about two decades worth of favors.

Now, I just need to tell her.

"You have your birth certificate, right?" I ask as I strip off the remains of yesterday's clothes.

Adina blinks up at me, brow furrowed. "Yeah, I had to get it to enroll in school. Why?"

I pull a fresh pair of boxers up my legs. "We need it."

"Asher." She huffs impatiently, tugging the comforter over her bare chest and flopping back into the pillows. Sunlight catches in her hair, and something inside me tugs. "What is this about?"

I straighten up, temporarily distracted by how fucking beautiful she is. "My third request."

Her lips purse. "Are you being purposely infuriating?"

No, but maybe I should in the future, because watching her get all huffy with me is adorable. I grin as I take a clean T-shirt out of the closet and pull it over my head. "To be clear, you can say no. It won't change anything. I want you to know I'm in this, though, one hundred percent. No take backs." My pulse throbs as I move back to sit at the edge of the bed. "We're getting married. In about an hour."

The look of shock I get in response to this pronounce-ment is instant and perfectly predictable. "What!"

"We're getting married. Come on. I had Liam call in

some favors. There's a department store on the way that will have someone waiting to open early for us. You can get a dress, there's someone there to do makeup, and we can pick out rings." I feel my face split in a huge smile, beyond pleased with myself for pulling it off. "There will be a photographer and flowers waiting at City Hall. If you want to do a big thing, we can make that happen too. Maybe after you graduate?"

Her bottom lip trembles, and those beautiful green eyes are suddenly shining with tears. "It's only been, like, six weeks! People don't get married after six weeks!"

My answering smile is effortless, because she didn't say no. "We do. You have every right to be scared, Adina. A lot of people have let you down. I'm never going to be one of them, though, and this is the best way I can think of to show you I mean it. I'm not going anywhere, and I want you—*all of you*." I reach out to take her hand. "I'm going to make you so happy, angel. You just need to trust me."

Adina lifts a hand to press over her own mouth, like she's trying to keep herself from answering too quickly.

I feel so full right now, though, because I *know* her. She wants this every bit as badly as I do, and needs it in a way I'm only just beginning to understand.

We're getting married today, and I'm going to be her home, her safe space, and her anchor point when the world turns everything upside down.

I'm a man of science, but there's not a single part of me that doesn't believe in fate now. How could I not, when the evidence is right in front of me, staring at me like I'm insane? She's everything I never knew I needed, and living proof that I was wrong about my capacity to love someone more than myself.

"Angel." I laugh, reaching out to wipe away a single tear

that tracks down her cheek. "Not to rush you, but if we're going to do this, you'll need to put some pants on."

Her hand falls to her lap. "So, like... right now?" She half laughs, half cries.

"Right now," I confirm, grinning like a lunatic.

One second passes, then two.

"Oh, god." Her voice breaks, and then her entire face is scrunched up, trying to hold back tears. Then, my chest feels like it's going to burst, because she's *nodding*.

Holy shit.

"Is that a yes?" I demand incredulously, my heart leaping into my throat.

Adina sniffs, and nods again through the tears.

It's good enough for me. I'll take it.

With a whoop of excitement that's loud enough to wake the neighbors, I gather her face in my hands and kiss every inch of her tear-streaked skin. At some point, her sobs turn to laughs, and then we're both scrambling out of bed to get dressed.

Adina beams up at me as we go to leave the apartment, and I reach over her head to take the knit hat she forgot off the hook and pull it over her ears. We need to get going, but I can't resist stopping to stare at her, trying to memorize every last detail of this moment. It's the happiest of my life, hands down. There will be more because, though, because she's going to be my *wife*.

"Ready?" Her hand slips into mine, and then it's her pulling me out of the apartment, leading the way down to where a black town car is waiting to take us downtown.

"Yeah, angel," I finally answer, once we're tucked away together in the back seat. "I'm ready."

ADINA

6 MONTHS LATER

I GOT THE JOB.

I didn't expect to. At least, I wouldn't *allow* myself to expect to.

Somehow, even after six months of my life being pretty darn close to perfect, I couldn't bring myself to be optimistic about this. After all, if I didn't think I'd get the job, I could be happy and surprised if I did. If I *did* expect to get it and ended up *not* getting it, I'd have been devastated.

Incredibly, happy and surprised won out today, and I'm all but skipping as I get off at the familiar subway stop around the corner from Asher's office.

In the days when I haunted the place at night, I used to wonder about the people he worked with. Now, as I walk through the front door, I wave at the two women behind the reception desk, June and Dana. Ryan, the dental assistant, grimaces and promises to return the book he borrowed from me soon when I greet him in the back hall.

None of them know me as the girl who used to empty

their waste baskets. I'm just the woman their boss is in love with. *His wife.*

I find my adorable, lavender lab coat–wearing husband in his office, frowning at his computer screen. Asher looks up as I slip inside, closing the door behind me.

He pushes his chair back from the desk, face splitting in such a big smile that returning it is practically an involuntary response. "Come here."

I don't need to be asked twice. Crossing the room, I've barely cleared the corner of the desk before a pair of strong arms have wrapped around my waist, dragging me into a familiar, firm chest. Warmth spreads through my muscles, loosening tension I didn't even realize I was carrying just by being close to him.

Asher Roth is my happy place.

"Missed you," I murmur quietly, leaning down to meet his lips. Asher's arms tighten in response, pulling my body more firmly against his.

"Missed you too," he replies when we finally break apart, gazing up at me with such undisguised adoration it makes my heart flip. I'll never get used to being looked at like that; like I'm the most important person in the world, the most beautiful woman he's ever seen, and his very favorite person, all rolled into one. "How was your day?"

My smile widens. Getting the job was exciting and all, but telling Asher is even better. I bite my lip, savoring the anticipation for all of half a second before the news comes bursting out of me. "I actually got a call on the way over here... I got the job!"

Asher's face transforms instantly. "*You got it?*" The exclamation is so loud that I'm sure he can be heard out in the hall. I squeal when he leaps to his feet, pulling me off the ground with the force of his hug. "I'm so proud of you," he mumbles against my hair, and I sniff, burying my face against his neck.

This is such a full-circle moment for us. How could I have ever known that the kind dentist, who gave me a place to sleep on a snowy night, would be holding me in his arms, celebrating me achieving my dream at the end of it all. For years, I've thought about how lucky I was that day. My bad luck had finally run out, and I ended up in the right place at the right time.

How could I have possibly known that *lucky* was such a spectacular understatement?

My eyes are burning as Asher sets me down on the edge of his desk and gathers my face in his hands to kiss me with such obvious devotion that it makes my throat tighten.

How is it even possible to love someone this much?

"It's per diem to start," I tell him when we break apart, our foreheads still pressed together as we beam at each other. "The money isn't awesome, but apparently they have a few full timers retiring this year, so who knows." My smile fades a little as a sliver of worry creeps in. "They warned me that paychecks might be a little all over the place the first few months—"

"That doesn't matter." Asher's voice is firm and leaves no room for argument. He shakes his head slightly, thumbs tracing back and forth over the sides of my face. "You're the love of my life, Adina Roth, and you've worked so incredibly hard for this. You're going to be spending your days *protecting children*. Do you really think I care how much money you're making?" His tone is incredulous, and his eyebrows lift in disbelief.

Well, when he puts it like that.

I sigh happily, feeling a smile pulling at the corners of

my mouth again as the last bit of doubt drains away. "I'm really excited. Like... *really* excited."

"You should be." His eyes glint behind his glasses. "Did I mention I'm proud of you? Ridiculously proud? It's obscene, really. I'll have to rent a billboard to shamelessly brag about how awesome my wife is."

Giggling, I lean forward to nip at his bottom lip. I adore goofy Asher. "You have mentioned it, I think."

"I'm going to say it a few more times too." Drawing back, he glances at his watch. "I have a few more appointments, but after that, we're going to dinner to celebrate."

It's been a hectic few months. The clinic has officially become a registered nonprofit, offering affordable dental care to low-income families in the city. Donations have been flowing in, and about a dozen local dentists have stepped up to volunteer their time on a regular basis. Every time I come here, there is new equipment being rolled in, fresh magazines scattered across the waiting room tables, and families drifting in and out with one less worry on their shoulders. There's already talk of expanding and opening other locations.

Asher doesn't make the calls anymore, but he doesn't seem to mind. There's a board of directors in charge of overseeing the budget, and the first thing they did was raise his salary to what a dentist living in one of the most expensive cities in the world should be making. Patients and parents love him, and I think they were worried about losing him.

I might be ridiculously proud too.

"I think I'd rather eat in tonight, Doctor Roth." My hands trail down his chest, coming to rest low on his abdomen as my mind drifts to *that one night* a few weeks ago. After the last of his staff had left for the night, the respectable doctor stripped me naked and fucked me in this exact place. All of our sex is incredible, but that particular night will live rent free in my head *forever*. Even now, weeks later, my skin is getting all hot and tingly just thinking about it.

He totally knows exactly what's on my mind, too, because the change in his demeanor is palpable. Lowering his head, he presses a chaste kiss to a place on my neck that makes me suck in an unsteady breath. "*Hmm*. I don't think so. I want to show you off, Mrs. Roth."

My head drops back, and I let out a noise somewhere between a laugh and a groan. I love hearing him call me that. "Asher..."

He's so mean. It'll be *hours* before we're alone. Which means I'll spend the evening walking around with wet panties that will *keep getting wetter* every time he brushes my arm or helps me into the back of a cab. Which is, of course, exactly what the asshole wants.

Me on my back—wet, desperate, and begging for him to fuck me—is Asher's very favorite thing. Unfortunately for both of us, right at this moment there are children in the neighboring exam rooms waiting for their dentist. Objectively, I know that the sooner he sees to his patients, the sooner we can leave. But the horny, emotional side of me, the one directly connected to my now aching pussy, doesn't want him to leave my sight.

With one last lingering kiss on my collar bone, he draws away, hands moving to adjust the length of his erection, which is straining against his pants. Not missing the way my eyes follow the motion closely, Asher chuckles throatily. "Patience, angel. You know I always take care of you."

I huff, wiggling off the desk. "You're a tease."

"I'll make it up to you." He leans back, staring at me for a moment. "I knew you'd get it. When we went to that work picnic last month, your internship supervisor was practically singing your praises."

It's fighting a losing battle to keep myself from looking too pleased.

"Go see your patients, Doctor Roth." I straighten his bow tie and kiss him gently, my whole heart full to bursting.

He grins, stealing another kiss before backing toward the door. "I want to take you away this weekend too. Let's get out of the city."

"Actually..." I bite my lip, cautiously excited about this other piece of information. "Some of the case workers invited me to sit with them at lunch a few times this week. I guess one of them, Elizabeth, is having a birthday party this weekend, and she invited me. It's just going to be a bunch of girls from the office."

Asher's smile widens. "You made friends."

I'm pretty sure my face is as red as a tomato right now, but I nod. "Don't make a big deal out of it," I say, knowing full well he's going to do exactly that. "They might still decide I'm a weirdo."

"You're putting yourself out there, angel!" He laughs. "You're amazing. Fuck, I really have to go. Wait here, I shouldn't be long. Maybe after dinner we'll stop somewhere? Get you something new to wear for the party?"

"Stop being so perfect. You're making me want to have sex with you."

He roars with laughter. "I'm trying to be worthy of my wife. Okay. I'm really going. Right now."

Despite saying that, he can't seem to resist walking right back to steal one more fierce kiss.

After he's gone, I stare around at the familiar walls, filled with feelings almost too big to contain. It doesn't escape me that this is the same room where a runaway teenage girl once laid on the couch, sobbing with grief and fear when she realized she wanted to be alive.

Sometimes, the grief for that lost girl hits me at the most unexpected times, but lately it's been less and less. Maybe it's because the good in my life has been canceling out the bad, or because I've managed to actually tell Asher when the weight of it threatens to drag me back under. Or, maybe, all the therapy my meddlesome husband insisted on for both of us is actually working.

Whatever the case, I'm pretty excited for whatever comes next.

* * *

Thank you so much for reading! If you enjoyed this story, please take the time to leave a rating or review. It is such an enormous help for indie authors like myself, and I genuinely love hearing people's thoughts on my work!

- Cleo

bonus epilogue

Want more of Asher & Adina? Download this free bonus epilogue and catch up with them five years after the end of this story.

afterword

As my brain is a mysterious, twisty place filled with trick steps, fake doors and lots of nonsensical decoration, Age of Shade began as a forced proximity, Hanukkah romance. As I started writing, though, a completely different story came out and I wouldn't have it any other way. Asher and Adina (named by my long-suffering beta reader Anya, who has dealt with this nonsense almost from the start) took on a life of their own, and here we are.

Thank you to all the people who supported me while writing this, including my family (who will never read this book. Ever.), my friends (who will gleefully text me their thoughts on the blowjob scene), but especially my husband who has unconditionally loved and encouraged me through every bought of self doubt, imposter syndrome, defeat and exhaustion. I can never thank you enough for believing in me and my smutty books. I love you. You're my favorite person.

Admittedly, I am writing this before sending it off to my amazing editor/friend/fellow ADHD gremlin Lauren, but

I'm 99.9% confident you're going to do an incredible job, so a huge thank you in advance for that.

Another big thank you to my beta readers, Anya, Dani, Mandy & Meagan for your invaluable advice and for lending me your dirty minds. This story wouldn't be what it is without you.

Although I definitely feel like I've said "thank you" too many times in this, I'm going to fight through the gnawing discomfort to offer another very large thank you to my ARC readers. THANK YOU. You guys are the unsung heroes of the publishing world, and amazing humans for dedicating your time to helping books like this one be seen.

Okay! I'm done! Thank you—*oh fuck, not another one*—for sticking with me through this!

Cleo White's affinity for all things dark, dramatic, and hopelessly romantic began the day she was born, which happened to be in the middle of a record-breaking snowstorm on Valentine's Day. Her love of literature came soon after, and she spent the better part of her childhood with both a book and a notebook full of unfinished stories in hand. Later in life, she found a love of writing spicy books with complicated characters and dysfunctional family drama. Cleo currently lives in Vermont with her husband and two daughters. When not writing, she can be found hiking, gardening, painting, and consuming excessive quantities of caffeine.

To stay up to date with upcoming releases and receive exclusive bonus content, subscribe to my newsletter at www.cleowhite-books.com

also by cleo white

In the mood for more forbidden insta-love, age-gap, spicy goodness?
Check out Cleo's other books!

Out of Sight

In Pieces

Age of Shade

You're It

Personal Matters

The Storm

One More Time

For Always

End Game

Silver Fox A-Listers Series

Actor

Artist

Rocker